Born [...] caree[...] short stories. He found success early and many of his short stories were published in magazines, including *The New Yorker, Harper's* and *Playboy*. Practically all of his short fiction has been collected in various volumes.

During World War II Shaw served as a private, then as a Warrant Officer in North Africa, the Middle East and all over Europe. Drawing on first-hand observations, he published his first novel, THE YOUNG LIONS, after the war and achieved instant acclaim. He has now written more than a dozen novels all of which are worldwide bestsellers. They include RICH MAN, POOR MAN and its sequel BEGGARMAN, THIEF; TWO WEEKS IN ANOTHER TOWN, EVENING IN BYZANTIUM, BREAD UPON THE WATERS and ACCEPTABLE LOSSES. His books have been enormously successful as feature films and TV serials and have been translated into twenty languages. Today the author divides his time between New York and Switzerland.

RETREAT
and other stories
Irwin Shaw

NEW ENGLISH LIBRARY

ACKNOWLEDGEMENTS

Some of the stories included in this collection have already appeared in
magazine form:
I STAND BY DEMPSEY, copyright 1939, by *The New Yorker*. STOP
PUSHING ROCKY, THE DEPUTY SHERIFF, THE GREEK
GENERAL, copyright 1938, by *The Crowell Publishing Company*
RESIDENTS OF OTHER CITIES copyright 1939, by
Esquire-Coronet Inc.

First published in the United States of America by Random House.
Copyright 1937, 1938, 1939, 1940, 1941, 1942, 1943, 1944, 1945, 1946
by Irwin Shaw

First NEL Edition April 1970
New edition November 1977
New edition February 1978
New edition February 1979
Reprinted July 1984
Reprinted July 1985

NEL Books are published by
New English Library,
Mill Road, Dunton Green, Sevenoaks, Kent.
Editorial office: 47 Bedford Square, London WC1B 3DP

Made and printed in Great Britain by
Hunt Barnard Printing Ltd., Aylesbury, Bucks.

0 450 00480 5

Contents

Publisher's Foreword

Irwin Shaw has established a reputation as one of the leading American literary figures of this century with such critically-acclaimed best-sellers as THE YOUNG LIONS and TWO WEEKS IN ANOTHER TOWN, and for his short stories, for example, TIP ON A DEAD JOCKEY. This present collection of his early short stories gives a fascinating view of a major author embarking upon his writing career.

The unmistakable, polished prose style demonstrated in his later, lengthier works is here revealed in a different context as he skilfully applies it to one of the most demanding of literary creations – the short story.

None of the stories in this collection has, in fact, been published in England before and its first publication must surely represent something of a literary event – which can only increase the following of this most outstanding and excellent author.

RETREAT

The column of trucks wound into the little square beside the Madeleine and stopped there, under the trees. They were furry with dust, the black cross almost indistinguishable even in the bright Paris sunlight under the harsh dry coat they had accumulated in the retreat from Normandy.

The engines stopped and suddenly the square was very quiet, the drivers and the soldiers relaxing on the trucks, the people at the little tables in the cafés staring without expression at the line of vehicles, bullet-scarred and fresh from war against the trees and Greek columns of the Madeleine.

A major at the head of the column slowly raised himself and got out of his car. He stood looking up at the Madeleine, a dusty, middle-aged figure, the uniform no longer smart, the lines of the body sagging and unmilitary. The major turned around and walked slowly toward the Café Bernard across the square, his face grimy and worn and expressionless, with the dust in heavy, theatrical lines in the creases of his face and where his goggles had been. He walked heavily, thoughtfully, past his trucks and his men, who watched him dispassionately and incuriously, as though they had known him for many years and there was nothing more to be learned from him. Some of the men got out of their trucks and lay down in the sunshine on the pavement and went to sleep, like corpses in a town where there has been a little fighting, just enough to produce several dead without doing much damage to the buildings.

The major walked over to the little sidewalk tables of the Café Bernard, looking at the drinkers there with the same long, cold, thoughtful stare with which he had surveyed the Madeleine. The drinkers stared back with the guarded, un-

7

dramatic faces with which they had looked at the Germans for four years.

The major stopped in front of the table where Segal sat alone, the half-finished glass of beer in his hand. A little twist of a smile pulled momentarily at the German's mouth as he stood there, looking at Segal, small and pinned together with desperate neatness in his five-year-old suit, his shirt stitched and cross-stitched to hold it together, his bald head shining old and clean in the bright sun.

'Do you mind . . . ?' the major indicated the empty chair beside Segal with a slow, heavy movement of his hand.

Segal shrugged. 'I don't mind,' he said.

The major sat down, spread his legs out deliberately in front of him. *'Garçon,'* he said, 'two beers.'

They sat in silence and the major watched his men sleeping like corpses on the Paris pavement.

'For this drink,' the major said, in French, 'I wanted to sit with a civilian.'

The waiter brought the beers and set them down on the table and put the saucers in the middle, between them. The major absently pulled the saucers in front of him.

'To your health,' he said. He raised his glass. Segal lifted his and they drank.

The major drank thirstily, closing his eyes, almost finishing his glass before he put it down. He opened his eyes and licked the tiny scallop of froth from the beer off his upper lip, as he slowly turned his head, regarding the buildings around him. 'A pretty city,' he said. 'A very pretty city. I had to have one last drink.'

'You've been at the front?' Segal asked.

'Yes,' said the major. 'I have been at the front.'

'And you are going back?'

'I am going back,' the Major said, 'and the front is going back.' He grinned a little, sourly. 'It is hard to say which precedes which. . . . . ' He finished his beer, then turned and stared at Segal. 'Soon,' he said, 'the Americans will be here. How do you feel about that?'

Segal touched his face uncomfortably. 'You don't really

8

want a Parisian to answer a question like that,' he said, 'do you?'

'No.' The major smiled. 'I suppose not. Though, it's too bad the Americans had to meddle. However, it's too late to worry about that now.' Under the warlike dust his face now was tired and quiet and intellectual, not good-looking, but studious and reasonable, the face of a man who read after business hours and occasionally went to concerts without being pushed into it by his wife. He waved to the waiter. '*Garçon*, two more beers.' He turned to Segal. 'You have no objections to drinking another beer with me?'

Segal looked across at the armored vehicles, the two hundred sprawling men, the heavy machine guns mounted and pointing toward the sky. He shrugged, his meaning cynical and clear.

'No,' said the major. 'I would not dream of using the German army to force Frenchmen to drink beer with me.'

'Since the Germans occupied Paris,' Segal said, 'I haven't drunk with one or conducted a conversation with one. Four years. As an experience, perhaps. I should not miss it. And now is the time to try it. In a little while it will no longer be possible, will it?'

The major disregarded the jibe. He stared across at his command stretched wearily and incongruously in front of the Greek temple Paris had faithfully erected in her midst. He never seemed to be able to take his eyes off the armor and the men, as though there was a connection there, bitter and unsatisfactory and inescapable, that could never really be broken, even for a moment, in a café, over a glass of beer. 'You're a Jew,' he said quietly to Segal, 'aren't you?'

The waiter came and put the two beers and the saucers on the table.

Segal put his hands into his lap, to hide the trembling and the terror in the joints of the elbows and knees and the despair in all the veins of the body that the word had given rise to in him, each time, every day, since the bright summer days of 1940. He sat in silence, licking his lips, automatically and hopelessly looking for exits and doorways, alleys and subway entrances.

9

The major lifted his glass. 'To your health,' he said. 'Come on. Drink.'

Segal wet his lips with the beer.

'Come on,' the major said. 'You can tell me the truth. If you don't talk, you know, it would be the easiest thing in the world to call over a sergeant and have him look at your papers. . . . '

'Yes,' said Segal. 'I'm a Jew.'

'I knew it,' said the major. 'That's why I sat down.' He stared at his men with the same look of bondage, devoid of affection, devoid of warmth or loyalty or hope. 'There are several questions in my mind you can answer better than anyone.'

'What are they?' Segal asked uneasily.

'No rush,' said the major. 'They'll wait for a minute.' He peered curiously at Segal. 'You know, it's forbidden for Jews to enter a café in France . . . ?'

'I know,' said Segal.

'Also,' said the major, 'all Jews are instructed to wear the yellow star on their coats. . . . '

'Yes.'

'You don't wear yours and I find you in a café in broad daylight.'

'Yes.'

'You're very brave.' There was a little note of irony in the major's voice. 'Is it worth it for a drink – to risk being deported?'

Segal shrugged. 'It isn't for the drink,' he said. 'Maybe you won't understand, but I was born in Paris, I've lived all my life in the cafés, on the boulevards.'

'What is your profession, Mr. . . . ? Mr. . . . ?'

'Segal.'

'What do you do for a living?'

'I was a musician.'

'Ah,' there was an involuntary little tone of respect in the German's voice. 'What instrument?'

'The saxophone,' said Segal, 'in a jazz orchestra.'

The major grinned. 'An amusing profession.'

10

'I haven't played in four years,' said Segal. 'Anyway, I was getting too old for the saxophone and the Germans permitted me to make a graceful exit. But imagine, for a jazz musician, the cafés are his life, his studio, his club, his places to make love, his library and place of business. If I am not free to sit down on a *terrasse* and have a *vin blanc* in Paris, I might just as well go to a concentration camp. . . . '

'Every man,' said the major, 'to his own particular patriotism.'

'I think,' said Segal, starting to rise, 'that perhaps I'd better go now. . . . '

'No. Sit down. I have a little time.' The German stared once more at his men. 'We will arrive in Germany a half hour later, if at all. It doesn't matter. Tell me something. Tell me about the French. We have not behaved badly in France. Yet, I feel they hate us. They hate us, most of them, almost as much as the Russians hate us. . . . '

'Yes,' said Segal.

'Fantastic,' said the major. 'We have been most correct, within the bounds of military necessity.'

'You believe that. It's wonderful, but you really believe it.' Segal was beginning to forget where he was, whom he was talking to, the argument rising hot within him.

'Of course I believe it.'

'And the Frenchmen who have been shot . . . ?'

'The army had nothing to do with it. The S.S., the Gestapo . . . '

Segal shook his head. 'How many times I have heard that!' he said. 'And all the dead Jews, too.'

'The army knew nothing about it,' the major said stubbornly. 'I, myself, have never lifted my hand, or done one bad thing against any Jew in Germany or Poland or here in France. At this point, it is necessary to judge accurately who did what . . . '

'Why is it necessary?' Segal asked.

'Let us face the facts.' The major looked around him suddenly, lowered his voice. 'It is very probable now that we are beaten . . . '

11

'It is probable,' Segal smiled. 'It is also probable that the sun will rise sometime about six o'clock tomorrow morning.'

'A certain amount of revenge – what you call justice, will be demanded. The army has behaved in a civilised manner and that must not be forgotten.'

Segal shrugged. 'I do not recall seeing the Gestapo in Paris until after the German army came in. . . . '

'Ah, well,' said the major, 'you are not representative. You are a Jew, and naturally a little more bitter, although you seem to have done very well, I must say.'

'I've done very well,' said Segal. 'I am still alive. It is true that my two brothers are no longer alive, and my sister is working in Poland, and my people have been wiped out of Europe, but I have done very well. I have been very clever.' He took out his wallet and showed it to the major. The Star of David was tucked in so that it could be snapped out in a moment, and there was a needle already threaded, wound round a piece of yellow cardboard right next to it. 'In a tight spot,' said Segal, 'I could always take out the star and put it on. It took six stitches, exactly.' His hand trembled as he closed the wallet and put it away. 'Four years, major, imagine four years praying each moment you will have thirty seconds somewhere to sew in six stitches before they ask to look at your papers. I've done very well. I've always found the thirty seconds. And do you know where I slept at night, because I was clever? In the woman's jail. So, when the Gestapo came to my house looking for me, I was comfortably locked in a cell among the whores and shoplifters. I could arrange that because my wife is Catholic and a nurse at the jail. Again, I've done very well. My wife decided finally she had had enough of me. I don't blame her, it's difficult for a woman. It's all right for a year, two years, but then the gesture wears out, you yearn not to have the millstone around your neck. So she decided to divorce me. A very simple procedure for a Christian. You merely go to court and say, 'My husband is a Jew,' and that's the end of it. We have three children, and I have not seen them for a year. Well enough. And the propaganda agencies, who also have no connection to the correct German army, also

12

have done well. The French hate the Germans, but they have been fed the lies for four years and I think maybe they will never quite get over the lies about the Jews. The Germans have various accomplishments to their credit, and this is another one . . . '

'I think perhaps you're being too pessimistic,' the major said. 'People change. The world goes back to normal, people get tired of hatred and bloodshed.'

'You're getting tired of hatred and bloodshed,' said Segal. 'I can understand that, after all this time.'

'Myself,' said the major, 'I never wanted it. Look at me. Fundamentally, I'm not a soldier. Come to Germany after the war and I'll send you a Citroën. I'm an automobile salesman, with a wife and three children, dressed in uniform.'

'Maybe,' said Segal. 'Maybe . . . Now we will hear that from many people. Fundamentally, I am not a soldier, I am an automobile salesman, a musician, a pet-fancier, a stamp-collector, a Lutheran preacher, a schoolteacher, anything. . . . But in 1940 we did not hear that as you marched down the boulevards. There were no automobile salesmen then – only captains and sergeants, pilots, artillerists . . . Somehow, the uniform was not such an accident in 1940.'

They sat silent. A passing automobile backfired twice, and one of the sleeping soldiers screamed in his sleep, the noise echoing strangely in the sunny square. One of the other soldiers woke the sleeping man and explained to him what had happened and the sleeper sat up against the truck wheel, wiped his face nervously with his hand, went to sleep again, sitting up.

'Segal,' said the major, 'after the war is over, it will be necessary to salvage Europe. We will have to live together on the same continent. At the basis of that, there must be forgiveness. I know it is impossible to forgive everyone, but there are the millions who never did anything. . . .'

'Like you?'

'Like me,' said the German. 'I was never a member of the Party. I lived a quiet middle-class existence with my wife and three children.'

13

'I am getting very tired,' Segal said, 'of your wife and three children.'

The major flushed under the dust. He put his hand heavily on Segal's wrist. 'Remember,' he said, 'the Americans are not yet in Paris.'

'Forgive me,' said Segal. 'I believed you when you told me I could talk freely.'

The major took his hand off Segal's wrist. 'I mean it,' he said. 'Go ahead. I have been thinking of these things for a long time, I might as well listen to you.'

'I'm sorry,' said Segal. 'I have to go home and it's a long walk, to the other bank.'

'If you have no objection,' said the major, 'I'll drive you there.'

'Thank you,' said Segal.

The major paid and they walked together across the square, in front of the men, who stared at them both with the same incurious, hostile expression. They got into the major's car and started off. Segal couldn't help enjoying his first ride in an automobile in four years and smiled a little as they crossed the Seine, with the river blue and pleasant below them.

The major barely looked at where they were going. He sat back wearily, an aging man who had been pushed beyond the limits of his strength, his face worn and gentle now with exhaustion as they passed in front of the great statues that guarded the Chambre des Députés. He took off his cap and the fresh wind blew his sparse hair in thin curls.

'I am ready to face the fact,' he said, his voice soft and almost pleading, 'that there is a price to be paid for what could be called our guilt. We have lost and so we are guilty.'

Segal chuckled drily. By this time he was feeling exhilarated by the beer he had drunk, and the ride, and the sense of danger and victory that came with talking to the major in a town full of German troops.

'Perhaps,' said the major, 'even if we hadn't lost we would be guilty. Honestly, Mr Segal, for the last two years I have thought that. In the beginning, a man is swept up. You have no idea of the pressure that is applied when a country like

14

Germany goes to war, to make a man join in with a whole heart, to try to succeed in the profession of soldiering. But even so, it wasn't the older ones like me . . . It was the young ones, the fanatics, they were like a flood, and the rest of us were carried along. You've seen for yourself. . . .'

'I've seen the young ones myself,' said Segal. 'But also the older ones, sitting at the best restaurants, eating butter and steaks and white bread for four years, filling the theatres, wearing the pretty uniforms, signing orders to kill ten Frenchmen a day, twenty . . .'

'Weakness,' said the major. 'Self-indulgence. The human race is not composed of saints. Somewhere, forgiveness has to begin.'

Segal leaned over and touched the driver on the shoulder. 'Stop here, please,' he said in German. 'I have to get off.'

'Do you live here?' the major asked.

'No. Five streets from here,' said Segal. 'But with all due respect, major, I prefer not showing a German, any German, where I live.'

The major shrugged. 'Stop here,' he told the driver.

The car pulled over to the curb and stopped. Segal opened the door and got out.

The major held his hand. 'Don't you think we've paid?' he asked harshly. 'Have you seen Berlin, have you seen Hamburg, were you at Stalingrad, have you any idea what the battlefield looked like at Saint Lô, at Mortain, at Falaise? Have you any notion of what it's like to be on the road with the American air force over you all the time and Germans trying to get away in wagons, on foot, on bicycles, living in holes like animals, like cattle in slaughter pens in an abattoir? Isn't that paying, too?' His face worked convulsively under the dust and it seemed to Segal as though he might break into tears in a moment. 'Yes,' he said, 'yes, we're guilty. Granted, we're guilty. Some of us are more guilty than the rest. What are we to do now? What can I do to wash my hands?'

Segal pulled his arm away. For a moment, helplessly he felt like comforting this aging, wornout, decent-looking man, this automobile salesman, father of three children, this weary, frightened, retreating soldier, this wavering, hopeless target on the straight, long roads of France. Then he looked at the rigid face of the driver, sitting at attention in the front of the car, with his machine pistol, small, and clever, well-oiled and ready for death in the sling under the windshield.

'What can I do?' the major cried again, 'to wash my hands?'

Segal sighed wearily, spoke without exultation or joy or bitterness, speaking not for himself, but for the first Jew brained on a Munich street long ago and the last American brought to earth that afternoon by a sniper's bullet outside Chartres, and for all the years and all the dead and all the agony in between. 'You can cut your throat,' he said, 'and see if the blood will take the stain out.'

The major sat up stiffly and his eyes were dangerous, cold with anger and defeat, and for a moment Segal felt he had gone too far, that after the four years' successful survival, he was going to die now, a week before the liberation of the city, and for the same moment, looking at the set, angry, beaten face, he did not care. He turned his back and walked deliberately toward his home, the space between his shoulder blades electric and attendant, waiting tightly for the bullet. He had walked ten steps, slowly, when he heard the major say something in German. He walked even more slowly, staring, stiff and dry-eyed, down the broad reaches of the Boulevard Raspail. He heard the motor of the car start up, and the slight wail of the tires as it wheeled around sharply, and he did not look back as the car started back toward the Seine and the Madeleine and the waiting troops sleeping like so many dead by their armored cars before the Madeleine, back along the open, unforgiven road to Germany.

PART IN A PLAY

Alexis Constantin was a pleasant man, and there were many people who thought he had talent, even before the war, when the theatre in Paris was crowded with good actors of his type, heavy, peasant-appearing men nearing middle age with an aptitude for shrewd comedy who could also be counted upon to be sympathetic and emotional when playing the aging rich husbands of flighty and unfaithful young women. He had been to Hollywood for a year or two and did an imitation of Boyer that was always amusing at parties. He had been married and amicably divorced when considerably younger and before the war had shared an apartment with Philippe Tournebroche, another actor, in the Saint Germain district. They had been friends ever since they had carried spears as young men together at the Odéon, and their friendship continued even though Tournebroche had become known as one of the most brilliant and successful actors in France before the Nazis came in and Constantin had merely plodded along, dependably, making a living, but always playing secondary parts, drawing a mildly approving paragraph from the reviewers here and there, but no more.

The actors' apartment was an agreeable place. Tournebroche made a great deal of money and was thoughtlessly open-handed with it. The two men got along together much better than either of them had got along with their wives, and there were a great many parties always going on there, with people from Broadway and Hollywood wandering through, and many bottles of champagne, and representatives of all the arts and always the new crop of pretty girls whom the two friends scrupulously shared, and a generous sprinkling of rich ladies and gentlemen with country places in Normandy and villas in

Cannes who could be counted upon when Paris turned dull. All in all, it was the sweet, rich, glorious life it was possible for an artist to live in the 1930s and which we are repeatedly warned will never return to the face of the earth.

Occasionally, when he was offered a part in a new play, Constantin would have his bad moments. 'The same thing,' he said one morning to Philippe, morosely leafing through a new script. 'Always the same thing.'

'Let me guess,' said Philippe. It was at breakfast, and Philippe was sitting across from him, meditatively tapping an egg. 'An industrialist. You manufacture perfumes.'

'Automobiles.'

'Automobiles. A play of superior quality. Your wife deceives you with an Italian.'

'A Hungarian. I have been cuckolded enough,' Constantin said bitterly, 'to have grounds for divorce against a nunnery full of English schoolgirls.'

Philippe grinned. 'Alexis Constantin,' he chanted oratorically, 'the eternal pillar of the French theatre. What would we do without the cuckold? The head reels at the thought. Pass the salt.'

'Some day,' Alexis said darkly, 'they are going to be surprised. They're going to offer me this part and I'm not going to take it. This isn't a career — it's a disease. . . . '

'Some day,' Philippe said gently, 'you're going to play Cyrano. I'm sure of it.' Philippe was sensitive and decent and he was very fond of Alexis, and as much as he could do to assuage the pain of disappointed ambition, he did.

But these were only the occasional moments, the flashes of dark clarity when Alexis saw his career slipping hurriedly past in a confused, unremembered succession of drab roles. He was not jealous of Philippe, or as little jealous as an actor can be, and there was always the human dream that next year would be different, a last-minute change in casting, a friend dying in a difficult and rewarding role and he called upon to fill in between matinee and evening performance; a peculiarly discerning producer suddenly appearing on the Parisian scene and calling him, saying, 'Constantin, I've been watching you. You've

18

been wasting yourself in those parts. I have here a new play in which the leading man runs from the age of nineteen to the age of eighty-five. He is irresistible to women and he is on the stage for two hours and twelve minutes. . . .'

But his friends never died, or died in bad roles; no discerning producers arrived in Paris; the pattern of his career was as even and predictable as wallpaper until the Germans entered Paris.

The Germans, who loved Paris much better than they loved Berlin, and who thought of themselves as connoisseurs and patrons of European are, interfered very little with the capital's theatre. Of course they closed down the plays written by Jews and handed Jewish-owned theatres over to more acceptable Frenchmen, for a price, and, naturally, they forbade the production of plays in which the English, Americans, or Russians were presented in a good light, but by and large they did no more harm to the theatre than a large motion-picture concern would do if given the same power.

The play Philippe was appearing in was a fiery story of the Franco-Prussian War, in which Frenchmen died eloquently on Uhlan lances in the third and fourth acts, so there was no question of its reopening. But Alexis was in one of his standard confections, acceptable to all parties except lovers of the theatre, and its producer was invited by the German Commissar of culture, a romantic Bavarian colonel, to put the play back on the boards.

'It's a problem,' Alexis was saying. He and Philippe had been talking around the subject all night. It was late now, and quiet outside, and there had been considerable brandy drunk over the problem.

'After all, I have only one profession. I am an actor.'

'Yes,' said Philippe. He was lying outstretched on the couch, staring into the brandy glass he held on his chest.

'A baker continues to bake. A doctor continues to practice medicine, Germans or no Germans. . . .'

'Yes,' said Philippe.

'After all,' Alexis said, 'the play is one that was a success under the Third Republic.'

'Yes,' said Philippe. 'That play was a success under Caligula.'

'It does no one any harm.'

'Yes,' said Philippe. 'Pass the brandy.'

'There is nothing in it to give comfort to the Nazis.'

'Yes,' said Philippe.

There was a pause. From the street came the sound of marching, three or four men only, but the hobnails hit the pavement like an army.

'The Germans,' said Philippe. 'They march to weddings, assignations, toilets. . . .'

'Are you going to play this season?' Alexis asked.

Philippe rolled the liquor around in his glass. 'I am not going to play this season,' he said.

'What are you going to do?' Alexis asked.

'I'm going to drink brandy,' said Philippe, 'and read the collected works of Molière.'

Alexis listened to the marching dying away in the direction of Montparnasse.

'Are you going to play next season?' he asked.

'No,' said Philippe. 'I am going to play the season the only Germans in Paris are dead Germans.'

'You don't think it's right, even in a play like mine . . .?'

Philippe waved his glass slowly past his nose. 'Each man has to decide for himself. I am not going to influence anyone on a question like this.'

'You don't think it's right?' Alexis persisted.

'I . . . .' Philippe spoke slowly and softly into the large, delicate glass. 'I think it's treason. I am not in the market as an entertainer for the brave, blond German troops.'

The two friends remained in silence. From the street came a hoarse voice, bellowing a Schubert *lied*, and a woman's high giggle.

'Well,' said Alexis finally, 'I'll call Lamarque in the morning and tell him he has to find someone else for the part.'

Philippe slowly put down his glass. He got up and came over to where Alexis was sitting. For the first time since the Germans had entered the city, Alexis saw emotion breaking through the bored, remote, cold mask of Philippe's famous face. With surprise, Alexis saw that Philippe was crying. Philippe held out his hand.

'I was afraid,' he said. 'I was afraid you wouldn't. . . . Forgive me, Alex, forgive me. . . . '

They shook hands, and Alexis was surprised again to see that he, too, had tears in his eyes as he clasped the hand of this man he had known for twenty years.

For a while it was not so bad. The Germans were correct, especially to well-known people in the theatre, and Alexis and Philippe remained aloof, pretending to be taking their time finding suitable parts, politely rejecting all manuscripts offered them. Philippe had a good deal of money, which he shared unstintingly with Alexis. They had a kind of prolonged vacation, reading, lying abed late, even spending seasons in the country after arming themselves with passes which were given graciously and without question by the Germans. There were long, quiet parties now at the apartment, at which painters showed new work which they refused to exhibit publicly, and playwrights read new plays that were meant for the boards sometime in the hazy future when the Germans were finally cleared out of Paris. That time, as the occupation wore on, seemed more and more dreamlike and impossible of achievement, and occasionally men and women of their circle would drop out and take once more their accustomed places on the stage, making their separate peace with the fact that the stalls were packed with German troops, in Paris on leave as a reward for their work on the various fronts.

The holiday began to pall on both Alexis and Philippe, especially as new faces appeared on the Parisian stage, new favorites claimed the attention of the public. Also, Philippe's money gave signs of running out and the Germans confiscated their apartment and they were forced to live, both of them together, in a small room on the fifth floor of a building without an elevator on a bad street in the Saint Denis section.

Finally, there was the day Lamarque sent a note to Alexis. He wanted to see Alexis alone and he wished Alexis to keep quiet about it for the time being.

Alexis dressed carefully for the interview, his best remaining suit, and a sober, expensive necktie he hadn't worn in two years. He had his hair cut on his way to Lamarque's office, and just before he went up the stairs bought a flower for his buttonhole. He mounted the stairs slowly, a solid, fleshy, handsome citizen, his face somber and reserved, hiding the sharp, nervous pangs of excitement and premonitory guilt as he opened the door of the producer's office.

'Germans or no Germans,' Lamarque was saying, 'this play' – he waved the manuscript excitedly above his desk – 'this play is theatrical literature. It's a contribution to the culture of France. And the leading part . . . My God!' Lamarque looked religiously up to heaven. 'An old man, but powerful, in the full flush of his maturity, on the stage half the first act, the whole second act, and a death scene in the third act Racine couldn't have done better.' Lamarque was a little fat man from Marseilles with small, shrewd, dark, promoter's eyes. He had done well under the Third Republic, he had done well under the Germans, and he would do well under the Ninth Dictatorship of the Proletariat.

'Alexis,' he gripped the actor's arm fiercely, 'Alexis, when I read this I could only think of one man. You. I know the trash you've been playing. The same old thing, year after year. Same tricks, same notices. Death for an actor. This would be a new Constantin. Raimu, Bauer, they'll seem like schoolboys next to you. I've always felt that when the right part came along you could astonish the world.'

'It's true,' Alexis said tentatively, knowing that it was only because so many of the old standbys were no longer playing that Lamarque was talking to him, 'I have somehow not had the opportunity to . . .'

'This is it, Alex,' Lamarque said solemnly. 'Believe me I've been in the theatre all my life and I know when a part and an actor get together like electricity.'

'However,' Alexis said, in a troubled voice, 'it's very kind of you, but in a way, I thought I'd wait for awhile. . . .'

'He's a miser,' Lamarque said reverently. 'A huge, powerful

22

miser. He's the hard-fisted, ruthless, scheming king of an industrial empire, with a pathologic love for money. He was disappointed in love in his youth and he has turned from women. All his passion is given to his money. His money is his wife, his mistress, his children, his life, and he ruins men with a laugh for a thousand francs. There's a scene when his best friend comes to him and pleads . . . but you have to read it for yourself, Alex, the power, the power, I don't want to spoil it for you. And there's a pure young girl he meets . . . And his change. The blossoming in December, the laughter. And then the discovery. The girl's a slut. Off with a captain in the Algerian cavalry at the moment he is buying a large pure diamond in a simple setting for her in the Place Vendôme. And a mad scene, Alex, a mad scene that makes *Hamlet* look like a game of dominoes on a Sunday afternoon. And the murder and the speech before he takes the poison! And the bloody, raging prayer to his God, with the glass in his hand! Alex,' he said solemnly, 'as God is my judge, this is the time for you to take your place in the history of the French theatre. . . . Here!' He thrust the manuscript into Alexis' hand. 'Don't say another word. Take it with you and read it, and come back to me at five o'clock this afternoon and take my hand and say, 'Lamarque,I want to thank you from the bottom of my heart. I am ready for rehearsals tomorrow morning!'

A little dazedly, Alexis left the office. He walked slowly toward the Seine and sat down on one of the benches overlooking the river, and in the pale spring sunlight read the play.The play was written with bite and energy, and was not as lurid as Lamarque had described it, although it was studded with big, showy scenes for the principal character. As he stared unseeingly across the river, Alexis could imagine himself striding a richly lit stage, cruel, monstrous, pitiful, torn, charming, stricken, corrupt, murderous, suicidal, evil, calling down the powers of hell upon the world he was leaving behind him.

It was a role the vision of which had haunted his dreams ever since he had first set foot on a stage, and Alexis knew, as he walked slowly toward his apartment, that whatever Philippe would say, he was going to take it. . . .

It was a great success. Overnight his name became a tradition in the French theatre. The comic, aging cuckold was forgotten, and in his place was a tragic actor of historic stature. Every new script of any importance was submitted to him and he did two films in the suburbs that made his face famous throughout Europe. It was true that several of his more hot-headed friends cut him on the street and there were one or two savage articles about him in some of the flimsy resistance sheets that were unkindly sent to him and, of course, Philippe had broken with him, on that first afternoon. . . .

'Yes, yes,' Philippe had said wearily, 'I know all the arguments. Argument one : we must eat. Argument two : the baker bakes, the doctor medicines, etc. Argument three : the Germans have won and will continue to win. Are we to make no arrangements for the rest of our lives? Argument four : we all know French misers, must we only present Frenchmen as angels, etc? Argument five : I'm through with you.'

And Philippe had packed and that was the last Alexis had seen of him. Later, he heard vaguely that Philippe was serving with the maquis in the Haute Savoie, and on one or two occasions had even been glimpsed in Paris, looking considerably older and shabbier than he had before. Alexis suffered a twinge of uneasiness each time he heard Philippe had been seen in Paris, but he was busy and successful and honored on all sides and consolation came easy.

It was in July, 1944, when Alexis next saw Philippe. The Americans were at Saint Lô, and Paris had become an uneasy city, tremors of guilt and joyful anticipation running through its secret life. Shots were heard in the streets at night, the Germans strode through the city searching the eyes of the inhabitants, calculating and puzzled; other Germans were found obscurely murdered along the river or floating face down toward the sea. Everyone knew that resistance battalions had been formed and the seventeen-year-old child who cleared the dishes from your table in a restaurant might be a Communist captain with an arsenal under his mattress and your name quite possibly on his list for retribution. Among the who had done well under the Germans, or who had done nothing against them, there was a quiet, nervous, unhappy adding up of interior accounts. Alexis was no exception. He was not playing at the time and he took to long slow, speculative walks and sitting up late and alone at night, staring out the dark windows of his apartment at the waiting, trembling city around him. He followed the war maps closely, and examined his reactions as honestly as he could, and was pleased to see, that despite the danger to himself, he felt a thin, undeniable thrill of joy when the Americans broke through in Normandy and clearly took the road to Paris.

Philippe, when he saw him near the Etoile, was almost unrecognizable. He had grown much older, with gray hair and deep furrows in a face that had become very thin and weather-beaten. This, added to his clumsy clothes and heavy boots, made him seem like a farmer, and a poor one at that, committed to a bleak ten acres of unprofitable land, in town for a day. Alexis walked behind him, watching, and noticed painfully the harsh, wounded limp with which Philippe moved past the little tables of the cafés.

For a moment Alexis almost stopped, feeling that he must avoid this scarred, bitter-seeming veteran. But looking at the awkward, weathered, familiar back, thinking of the twenty years of friendship, twisted in the uncertain guilty currents of that bloody August, he walked more quickly, overtook Philippe, put his hand on his arm.

Philippe stopped, looked around. There was a quick, momentary tightening around his eyes, but that was all. 'Yes, monsieur?' he asked politely.

'Please, Philippe,' Alexis begged. 'Don't say monsieur.'

Philippe started to pull his arm away.

'Please talk to me. . . . ' But Philippe began to walk away, deliberately, but not slowly, before the café tables.

Alexis followed him. 'I'm sorry,' he said. 'I was a fool. I was weak. Anything you say. I should have gone with you. I've heard of what you've been doing. I'm proud you were once my friend.'

Philippe limped slowly along, looking straight ahead, as though he heard not a word.

'Anything,' Alexis said, pleadingly. 'I'm ashamed of myself. I have a lot of money. I know you people need it. Take it. All of it.'

For the first time a look of interest came into Philippe's face. He glanced sidelong at his friend, speculatively.

'Money buys guns,' Alexis said hurriedly. 'Everyone knows the Germans sell guns, but expensive . . . You haven't got the right to turn me away. No matter what you think of me. I want to do something to help. Maybe it's late, but I want to help. Myself, too. There'll be fighting. I'm willing to fight. Forget the last three years. At least, now, for the time being, forget . . .'

Philippe stopped. He stared coldly, without friendship at Alexis. 'Don't talk so loud,' he said.

'Forgive me,' said Alexis humbly.

'And get out of here and go back to your home. And wait there.'

'Will you come there?' Alexis asked happily.

'Maybe.' Philippe shrugged, smiled sourly. 'Maybe we will.'

'My address is . . .'

'We know what your address is. Good-bye, monsieur.' Without a smile, without a handshake, Philippe walked off. Alexis looked after the harsh, limping figure losing itself among the bright dresses, and the bicycles and the green uniforms in the sunlight, feeling sick for the lost twenty years, but also feeling a quickening and a hope he had not felt for months. He turned and went back to his apartment and sat there and waited.

'This gentleman,' Philippe was saying, his voice touched with a light, scornful amusement, the first sign Alexis had seen of the long years this civilian soldier had spent on the stage, 'this gentleman is known to me.'

There were three of them who had come up to Alexis' apartment with Philippe just after dark. They were small, quiet men, very young, shabby and deadly-looking, and Alexis felt himself being weighed candidly and swiftly in their steady glances, as they sat across from him in his bright, comfortable living room.

'Early in the Occupation,' Philippe went on, 'he turned himself over to the service of the Germans, as so many did. . . .'

Alexis opened his mouth to protest, to say that continuing at his profession, keeping a theatre lit, in French, even though Germans did attend, was not so irrevocably sinful, especially when measured against the full-hearted co-operation so common in other and more important fields – but looking at the four, cool, quiet faces, he decided merely to sit there and remain silent.

'Now' – there was a slight stagey, amused mockery in Philippe's voice – 'now the Americans are in Rennes and this gentleman has suffered a new growth of patriotism. . . .'

'Philippe,' Alexis protested regretfully, 'May I talk for myself?'

One of the other men nodded.

'I was wrong,' Alexis said. 'I wish to make up for it. Money. As much as I have. Myself, if I can be of assistance. It's as simple as that.'

The three men looked at each other. Philippe turned his back, stared at a Derain drawing on the wall.

One of the men stood up, came over and shook Alexis' hand. The others smiled at him a little, with a touch of warmth, but Philippe didn't look at him, even when he took out the huge pile of franc notes and turned them over. Philippe did not say good night when he left.

When the fighting started in the city, at barricades and windows and on the roofs, they called for Alexis and he went with them, in old flannels, that he had used to lounge on the beach at Cannes, with the new armband that marked him as a member of the French Forces of the Interior. In the crowded room near the Hotel de Ville, waiting to receive what arms were available, with the preliminary crackling of automatic fire coming in through the windows, he looked again and again at the badge of acceptance on his arm. He felt too old for this and fear was a stone lump at the back of his throat and he was ashamed that his shirt was stained with nervous sweat, but when he looked down at the mark on his arm, there was a sense of religion and peace that almost compensated for the cold trembling nerves and the pumping blood.

They gave him four potato-masher grenades, which he stuck in his belt, after surreptitiously watching what the other men did with theirs, like a country cousin at a banquet watching the host pick up knives and forks.

Philippe came in and the room fell silent. Philippe stood before them and spoke in a low, even voice. 'We do not intend to fight pitched battles at this point,' he said. 'We will harass them, pick them off when we can, try to make them stay and take cover and hole up until the Americans get here. We will try to make it expensive for them to move anywhere in Paris. We will be frugal with ammunition and weapons. I am sorry we are not better armed. Anyone who feels that he is not well enough equipped to go into this engagement is at liberty to leave. . . . ' He looked thoughtfully at Alexis as he spoke. Alexis stroked the handle of one of the grenades.

Philippe came over and stood before him. 'Monsieur,' he said, 'do you know how to use your weapon?'

'I – uh . . . Not exactly.'

Philippe pulled one of the grenades out of Alexis' belt and showed him how to hold it, how to withdraw the pin, how to throw it. Alexis thanked him and Philippe gave him back the grenade and spoke sharply to all of them. 'All right. We are ready. . . . '

They slid out into the night.

The next two days were a confused series of clanging dreams for Alexis; the first, bitting smell of powder, the sharp, malicious chips of stone flying off window sills past your head and the mean, continuing searching noise of German machine guns, and a man falling beside you with a bullet through his lung and your taking his 1918 rifle and firing into the dust a hundred yards away and perhaps hitting the running gray figure there; and the heavy-footed trotting from one barricade of stones and tree trunks to another, with the inexorable noise

28

of the Tiger tank turning the corner behind you and churning through the debris, and the hopeless, dissolving sound of shells hitting around you and the bloody disintegration before your eyes when the overturned car in front of you was hit by a shell and the two men and a woman pinned under it vanished . . . The boys around him were pleased with him and called him 'Poppa' and loyally swore one of his grenades had fallen inside a tank turret when he dropped it from a third-floor window near the Opera and from time to time, in little flashes in the heat and fear and exhaustion, he was pleased with himself and surprised that there was so much of the soldier hidden under the boulevardier and artist. Philippe alone spoke to him coldly and professionally, not discriminating against him, but showing him no favor. Alexis did not mind. In the ambush and counter ambush, in the sudden burst from the roof, and the dry-mouthed stalking down the moonlit streets, there was no time to think of anything except the next German, the nearest cover, a hurried sip of wine to dissolve for an instant the stone of thirst and terror in the throat, a place to lie down and sleep for an hour to keep from dying of fatigue on your feet. . . .

He was alone with Philippe, hiding behind a wooden door that was just open a slit, so they could cover the street. Seven men of the group had just left them, going down the street to investigate the report that there were four or five Germans hiding in a wine merchant's cellar half a block away.

He could hear Philippe breathing hard beside him, because they had run a hundred yards down the broad street to get here, with two shots fired at them from snipers on the roofs. There were strange, wonderful colored gyrations of the atmosphere before his eyes and he heard his breath coming like the noise of some ancient machine, creaking and in need of oil. He sank to one knee, leaning against the door, feeling the door get wet from the sweat that was thick on his forehead. For a moment, looking up at the gaunt, red-eyed, scarred, be-stubbled face above him, wavering in the gyrating lights of his own exhaustion, he thought of Philippe and himself sitting across from each other, many years before at breakfast, the coffee steaming between them, the newspapers fresh and black before them, themselves newly washed in crisp silk robes. . . . 'Your wife,' Philippe had said jokingly at breakfast a long time ago, 'deceives you with an Italian. . . .'

'They're going too slow. Too slow,' Philippe was looking out the door. He had opened it wider and was watching his patrol cautiously make its way, hugging the sides of the buildings toward the wine merchant's cellar. 'Stay here,' he said to Alexis. 'I've got to get them to move faster. . . . ' He looked down at Alexis curiously. 'Are you all right?' he asked.

With an effort, Alexis got to his feet, essayed a smile. 'Sure,' he said. 'I'm a little old for this sort of thing. That's all.'

'Yes,' said Philippe and slipped out after the patrol.

He had only been gone five seconds when Alexis saw the truck. It ground around the corner and stopped for an instant at the end of the street. It was a big open German army truck, with a machine gun mounted on it above the driver's cab in front, and it seemed to be full of men, with rifles bristling on all sides.

Alexis threw open the door. 'Philippe!' he screamed.

Philippe turned and he and the men of the patrol saw the truck just at the moment that the truck driver and the man at the machine gun saw them. The Frenchmen started to run and the driver threw his vehicle into gear and picked up speed, pursuing them. The machine gunner fired several bursts, but the jolting of the truck made him wild and the bullets ricocheted around Philippe and the others as they ran toward the corner, where they would get a moment's respite. Alexis took one last look at Philippe, the limping, exhausted figure running grotesquely, rifle in hand, with stone chips and machine-gun bullets flickering around him. . . .

Alexis left the protection of the doorway and began to run across the street at an angle that would bring the truck even with him as it passed him. For a moment, no one in the truck saw him and he had time to pull the pin from a grenade as he ran heavily, diagonally, almost in the same direction as the careening truck, like a man running to swing on a trolley car. Then the machine gunner saw him and swung his weapon around at him. The first burst missed him and Alexis lumbered on, his breath singing weirdly in his ears, the grenade clutched tight in his sweating hand. The riflemen in the body of the truck saw him too, and the weapons appeared over the wooden sides, converging on him. Alexis never heard the shots, but he heard the sick whistle of the missiles past his head. One hit him high on the left shoulder and he stumbled, then picked himself up and, scrambling and stumbling, continued toward the approaching truck. The machine gunner swung his weapon around and there was the hysterical triphammer noise and Alexis felt something hit him in the head and there was the strange taste of blood in his mouth, although his tongue for some reason could not move to swallow it. He kept on, his shoes making a deliberate, shuffling, weary clatter on the pavement, amid all the other sounds, the grinding of the truck, the shots, the yelling German. His arms out to keep his balance, his legs moving with the insane deliberation of the mechanism of an automatic phonograph, staggering and sliding in his ruined fashionable flannels that had looked so well on the bright Mediterranean beach, blood streaming from his shoulder and head, leaving a plain dark wavering trail behind him on the pavement, his cheekbone exposed, broken and white in the bloody face, and the eye drooped close, its muscles torn and useless, and the other eye frantic and singed and dusty, he caught up with the rolling truck, put one hand on the cab, was dragged along for an instant while the man inside beat at the hand with the butt of his gun. With the homely, everyday grunt of a fat man swinging upon the platform of a suburban train, just reached in the morning, he pulled himself for a moment on to the running board and heaved the grenade up and over the wooden side into the mass of rifles and uniforms and ammunition and screaming men. . . .

He fell back and dropped peacefully to the pavement. Far off, it seemed to him, there was an explosion. Somehow he sat himself in the middle of the street and regarded his handiwork with the one crazy eye. The truck had overturned and was burning brightly. Here and there a gray uniform dragged itself painfully for a yard or two, but most of the gray uniforms lay still and some were still burning.

The ghost and spectre of a grin crossed what was left of his face.

Philippe walked slowly up to him. Alexis brokenly raised one arm to wipe the blood and stone dust out of his one eye so that he could see his friend more clearly. For a single mangled moment Alexis thought of the things that lay between them, the thousand drinks and the pretty girls and the vacations and the idle debonair hours after the theatre and the afternoon he had been no more than an actor and had decided to play the big, ludicrous, sinful part . . . The bloody mouth and the broken teeth mumbled something, lost in blood, and the single wild eye stared up, dying, begging forgiveness.

But Philippe said, gently, but coldly, 'Lie down, monsieur. We will look for the aid men.'

Alexis shook his smashed, tangled head, grieving, knowing in this last instant that he was unforgiven, and lay down on the stained and fractured pavement.

THE VETERANS REFLECT

The bells were ringing everywhere and the engineer blew the locomotive whistle over and over as they roared up the springtime valley. The hills rolled back from the blue river, and the frail green of the young leaves made them look as though pale green velvet cloth, thready and worn, had been thrown as drapery over their winter sides.

Peter Wylie sat at the window staring dreamily out at the Hudson Valley rolling sweetly and familiarly past him. He smiled when a little girl in front of a farmhouse gravely waved an American flag at the speeding train, and the engineer gravely saluted her in return with a deep roar of the whistle.

Peter Wylie sat at the window of the speeding train and avoided listening to the booming voice of the gentleman talking to the pretty woman across the aisle. He stretched his legs comfortably and half-closed his eyes as he watched the green, quiet country over which, faintly, between towns, came the pealing of bells, because that morning the war had ended.

'. . . Dead two years,' the gentleman was saying. 'His ship went down off Alaska and that was the last we heard of him. Twenty-one years old. Here's his picture, in uniform.'

'He looks so young,' the woman said.

'He had a blond beard. Hardly had to shave. The ship went down in eighteen minutes . . .'

The bells were ringing, Peter thought, and the graves were full of young men who had hardly had to shave, in uniform. His two cousins on his mother's side, killed in Africa, and Martin, who had been his roommate for three years, killed in India, and all the boys from the squadron . . . The graves on the plains and the mountains, the shallow graves on the hard coral islands, and the long well-kept cemetery of the military dead outside the hospital which you looked at through the tall window of your ward as nurses whispered outside in the corridor, and the doctors hurried fatefully by on their crepe soles. 'Convenient,' you said with a slow, remote wave of your hand and with what you hoped was a smile, to the nurse, who seemed always to have come from behind a screen where she wept continuously when not actually needed at a bedside. 'Modern design.'

'What?' the red-eyed nurse had asked blankly.

You had been too tired to explain and merely closed your eyes with the beautiful rudeness of the dying. But you hadn't died. There was a strong platter-like excavation in your abdomen and you would never really enjoy your food any more, and you would always have to climb stairs slowly even though you were only twenty-nine now on this day when the bells were ringing, but the cemetery and the military dead were still there, and here you were on a train up the Hudson Valley on your way home to see your wife and child, and the guns were quiet and the airplanes idled in the hangars, and the pilots sat around and played cards and tried to remember the telephone numbers of the girls in their home towns.

You were on your way home to see your wife and child. For three years, alone at night, sleepless in strange rooms on other continents; on leave, at a bar, sleepless, drinking and laughing, and the brassy old juke boxes playing songs that cried *far away and long ago, far away and long ago,* and all the women being earnest about the war and patriotically anxious to jump into bed with all the pilots, navigators, bombardiers, flight-sergeants, wing-commanders, meteorologists, radio-operators of the air forces of all the United Nations, including the Russian; for three years on the long droning flights across the hundred-mile ripples of the Pacific; for three years, even sometimes at the moment when the bombardier said, 'OK, I'll take it from here,' as the plane ducked in over the target and the anti-aircraft fire bloomed roughly about you, the faces of your wife and daughter slid through your mind, the woman's firm-boned jaw, the moody blue eyes, the wide, full mouth, familiar, loving, changing, merry, tragic, tenderly and laughingly mocking in the secret, wifely, female understanding of the beloved weaknesses of the man of the family — and the child's face, small, unformed, known only from photographs sent across the oceans, looking out at him through the night with sober, infant gravity. Three years, he thought, and tomorrow morning the train will pull into the dirty old station at Chicago and there they'll be, standing in the soot and clangor, hand in hand, the quick, delightful woman and the fat child, picking his uniform out among the other uniforms, with three years' waiting and loving and hoping showing in the faces as he strode down the platform. . . .

'Bong-bong!' shouted a little bald man, who was leading two women drunkenly down the aisle toward the diner. 'Bong-bong. We did it!'

'Ding-a-ling! Ring out the wild bells!' The blonde woman right behind the bald man cried out. 'Welcome to America!'

'We applied the crusher,' the bald man told the crowded car. 'The old steel spring technique. Coil back, coil back, coil back, then . . .'

They disappeared around the bend of the car over which the small sign said modestly, 'Women.'

Across the ocean, in the mountains of another country, a man strode out of a darkened house to the long, armored automobile waiting on the night-deserted road. Two men, bundled in army greatcoats, hurried behind him, their boots sighing softly in the damp earth of the courtyard. The chauffeur had the door open, but the man stopped and turned around before he got in and looked at the dark shapes of the mountains rising behind him against the starry sky. He put his hand uncertainly to his collar and pulled at it and took a deep breath. The two men in the greatcoats waited, without looking up, shadowed by the slowly fluttering young foliage of the oaks that bordered the path. The man turned and slowly got into the car, carefully, like an old man who has fallen recently and remembers that his bones are brittle and mend slowly. The other two men sprang into the front seat, and the chauffeur slammed the rear door and ran around to the front and leaped in and started the motor. The automobile sped quietly down the dark road, the noise of its going making a private and faraway *whoosh* that died on the huge and growing darkness of the mountain-circled spring night.

In the back of the car, the man sat bolt upright, his eyes narrow and unseeing, staring straight ahead of him. Off in the hills a church bell pealed and pealed again and again, musical and lonely in the echoing darkness. The lips of the man in the back seat curled slightly, bitterly, as the sound of the pealing village bell wavered on the wind. Germans! he thought. Five million Germans dead all over the world and the Russians on the road to Berlin and everything worse than 1918 and their leader skulking through the night on back-roads toward the Swiss border with a chauffeur and two frightened first-lieutenants and they ring bells as though this was the day after the Fall of France! Germans! Idiots! Imitation suits, imitation rubber, imitation eggs, finally imitation men . . . What was a man expected to do with material like that? And he'd come so close — so close . . . The gates of Moscow. But he sat. The statue sat. Everyone else ran, the diplomats, the newspapermen, the government, and Stalin sat there and the people sat . . . Peasant. Sitting there in his burning house with his gun and his plow — and somehow the house didn't burn. Storm-troopers, assault-guards, blitzkrieg veterans at the gates of Moscow and they died. A little cold and they dropped like hot-house violets. So close — so close . . .

The bell rang more strongly and in other villages other bells answered.

They'd hang him if they caught him. He'd cried at the last Armistice, he'd hang at this. . . . The British use a silk rope when they hang nobility. The wouldn't use silk on him. . . . And the bells ringing all around him . . .

He leaned forward and jabbed the chauffeur fiercely in the back.

'Faster!'

The car spurted forward.

'Production,' the booming gentleman across the aisle was saying to the pretty woman, who was leaning closer to him, prettily attentive. 'It was inevitable. American production won this war.'

Peter thought of the graves, of the English and Chinese and Australians and Russians and Serbs and Greeks and Americans who filled them, who had fought bitterly with rifle and cannon and plane across the torn fields and stripped forests where they now quietly lay, under the illusion that if the war was to be won, it was to be won by them, standing there, hot gun in hand, with the shells dropping around them and the scream of the planes overhead and the tanks roaring at them at fifty miles an hour. . . .

'I know,' the gentleman was saying. 'I was in Washington from 1941 right to the finish and I saw. I'm in machine tools and I had my hand on the pulse of production and I know what I'm talking about. We performed miracles.'

'I'm sure,' the pretty woman murmured. 'I'm absolutely sure.' She was not as young as she had looked at first, Peter noticed, and her clothes were much shabbier than he had thought, and she looked pretty and impressed and tired and ready to be invited to dinner.

'. . . Plants in seven states,' the man was saying. 'We expanded four hundred per cent. The war's over now, I can talk freely. . . .'

The war's over, Peter thought deliciously, settling deeper into his chair, and letting his head rumble pleasantly with the click of the wheels as he leaned back against the cushion, the war's over and machine-tool manufacturers who expanded four hundred per cent can talk freely to women in Pullman cars and tomorrow I see my wife and child and I never have to climb into an airplane again. From now on I walk down to the station and buy a ticket when I want to go some place and I sit down with a magazine and a whisky and soda and the train clicks along on steel and solid gravel and the only enemy activity will be an occasional small boy throwing a rock hopefully at the bright windows of the diner flashing by. Tomorrow afternoon he would be walking slowly along the lake front in the spring wind, hand in hand with his wife and child.

37

'And that, darling, is Lake Michigan. Do you know the water you took a bath in this morning? It comes right from here, especially for you. When your father was a boy he used to stand here and watch the red Indians sail by in their war canoes at forty miles an hour, reciting Henry Wadsworth Longfellow at the top of their voices. I can see by the look in your mother's eye that she doesn't believe me and wants an ice-cream soda. I can also see by the look in her eye that she doesn't think you should have an ice-cream soda so soon after lunch, but I've been thinking about buying you this ice-cream soda for three years and the war's over, and I don't think she's going to make too much of a fuss. . . .'

And tomorrow night, they would lie, soft on their backs in the soft bed, staring idly up at the dark ceiling, his arm under her head, their voices murmuring and mingling with the distant quiet night sounds of the sleeping city, the clack and rumble from the lakefront railroad yards and the soft whisper of automobiles on the highway. . . . 'I slept in the same bed in Cairo, Egypt, with a boy from Texas who weighed two hundred and thirty pounds. He wanted to get in the Navy, but he was six feet six inches tall and they said he wouldn't fit on any ship afloat or building. Also he was in love with a girl he met in New York who sold gloves in Saks and he talked about her all night long. She has a thirty-six inch bust and she lives with four girls from Vassar in Greenwich Village and she has a scar on her right buttock six inches long that she got when she fell down iceskating and a man with racing skates ran over her. This is an improvement over sleeping with a two-hundred-and-thirty-pound Texan in the same bed in Cairo, Egypt. Yes, I'll kiss you if you want . . .'

And her voice, close to his ear, in the gentle, tumbled darkness, alive with the fresh night wind off the lake and the familiar smell of her perfume and the frail dry smell of her hair, remembered all the years deep in his nostrils. '. . . And she went to the nursery school in Tucson all day while I was on duty in the hospital and they all liked her very much but she had a habit of hitting the other little boys and girls with her shovel and I had to leave her with my sister. I knew you'd laugh. Stop laughing or I'll stuff a pillow in your mouth, Mr Veteran. You can afford to laugh, out flying around ten thousand miles away with nothing to worry about but Japs and Germans. Wait till you're a mother and seven young mothers descend upon you to tell you your child has swiped at their children with a wooden shovel every day of the school term ... ' And the kiss to stop the laughter and her head under his chin after that and the slow, diminishing chuckles together for the child sleeping in the next room dreaming of other children and more wooden shovels.

And again, her hand thrown softly and possessively on his chest. 'There's a lot more hair here than I remember.'

'War. I always put on a lot of hair on my chest in a war. Any objections?'

'No. I'm well-known as a woman who's partial to hairy men. Or is talk like that too vulgar for young soldiers? Am I too fat? I put on eight pounds since 1942. . . . Have you noticed?'

'I'm noticing now.'

'Too fat?'

'Ummmmmmnnn ...'

'Tell the truth.'

'Ummnnn.'

'I'm going to diet. . . . '

'You just wait here and I'll go down and get you a plate of mashed potatoes. . . . '

'Oh, shut up! Oh, darling, darling, I'm glad you're home ...'

Or perhaps they wouldn't talk at all in the beginning. Perhaps they would just touch each other's hand and weep cheek to cheek for the three years behind them and the years ahead and cling to each other desperately through the long cool night and go to his parents' farm in Wisconsin and walk hand in hand in morning sunlight slowly over the greening fields, their feet sinking into the soft loam, content in the first hours with love and silence, until finally they could sit under the wide peaceful sky, off to themselves, with the rich smell of the newly plowed fields and the watermelon-cucumber smell of the

river in their nostrils, and then, finally, the words would come
. . . The things he had thought on the long flights, the de-
cisions and doubts of the thousand wartime nights, the deep,
deep hallelujah of his spirit as the train covered the sweet final
miles between the war and home. He would tell her the things
he had had to bury deep within him through the noisy, bleeding years . . . The times he had been afraid . . . the first time
he had seen the enemy squadron small against the horizon,
harmless-looking dots, growing nearer and larger with insane
speed, and the ridiculous way it made him see, over and over
again, for some reason, *Acrobatics*, as it was printed in the
March Field Bulletin. And at the time he had been shot, six
hours away from base, on a rough day, lying bleeding on his
parachute while Dennis pushed the bomber toward home, and
he had managed to keep quiet for the first four hours, but had
wept for the last two hours, almost mechanically, although he
had felt very calm. And because he was certain he was going to
die, he had for the first time permitted himself to think about
whether the whole thing was worth it or not, as the plane
bucked in the cold air. He could tell her now he had thought,
in those long six hours, of all the boys who had lightly roared
off at four hundred miles an hour and lightly and thoughtlessly, or at least silently died. . . . He would be able to tell
her that he had soberly decided, bullet in his belly and sure of
death in the roaring plane, that it was worth it, that if he had
to do it again he would leave home, wife, child, father,
mother, country, and search the German bullet out of the
cloud once more, part of the enormous anguish and enormous
courage of all the men on sea and beach and mountain locked
with him in final struggle against the general enemy. And,
then, weeping, on the edge of death, as he thought, he could
let himself go . . . and for the first time, in the mist of pain,
break down the barrier of reserve that had kept him, even in
his most secret thoughts, from admitting even to himself how
much he loved all those men behind guns – his friends, boys
from the same schools, coldly diving, cannons and machine
guns tearing out of their wings, at enemy bombers; the
pleasant Englishmen foolishly and desperately confident of
40

their ships, sailing formally and arrogantly into hopeless battle like Englishmen in books; the quilted Chinese rifleman standing forlornly on the brown China earth against tanks and artillery; and huge, muffled Russians, fighting by day and night and snow and rain, implacably and ingeniously and tirelessly killing, oblivious to agony or doubt, intent only on burning and crippling and starving and murdering the enemy. . . . He could tell her how deep inside him he had loved all those bloody, weary, cruel, reliable men, how he had felt borne up on that huge tide of men careless of death, and had felt himself to be part of that tide, agonised, stricken, familiar with defeat, often falsely and frivolously led, but better than the leaders, dangerous, brawling, indivisible – and how he had felt linked with those men for all their lives and his, closer to them even though he could not speak their language nor they his, than to his own mother and father, responsible forever for their comfort and glory as they were for his. And he could tell her of the sober exhilaration of these reflections, this deep dredging to his thoughts, this ultimate examination in the light of pain and exhaustion and terror of himself, who never before this had thought deeply or reflected much beyond the everyday cares of average life in a small town, seated at a desk from nine to five, sleeping comfortable in a quiet room in a warm house, going to the pictures twice a week, playing tennis on Sunday, worrying about whether the car was good for another year or not . . .

The long automobile sped down the winding road among the hills on its way through the night to the Swiss border. The man still sat bolt upright on the back seat, his eyes narrow and unseeing, straight ahead of him.

Victories, he thought, how many victories can a man be expected to win? Paris, Rotterdam, Singapore, Athens, Kiev, Warsaw – and still they kept coming. . . . There was a certain limit to the number of victories that were humanly possible. Napoleon discovered, too . . . Napoleon . . . Napoleon . . . He was tired of that name. In the last days he had ordered that it was not to be spoken in his presence. And now they were all hunting for him, like a world full of bloodhounds — Germans, English, Russians, Americans, French, Austrians, Poles, Dutch, Bulgarians, Serbs, Italians . . . Well, they had reason. Fools. For a long time it hadn't been hard. The cities fell like rotten apples. But then America and Russia . . . The timing was not quite exact. In politics everything happened before schedule. In war everything happened behind schedule . . . So close, so close . . . The Russians . . . Everything else being equal, the bells would be ringing for another reason tonight if not for the Russians . . . Just that winter had to be the coldest in fifty years. There has to be a certain element of luck. Well, all things considered, he had had a successful career. He had started out as a nobody, with his father always yelling at him that he'd never amount to anything and he never could hold a job . . . Today his name was known in every home on the face of the earth, in every jungle . . . Thirty million people had died earlier than they expected because of him and hundreds of cities were leveled to the ground because of him and the entire wealth of all nations of the earth had been strained by him, mines and factories and farms . . . All things considered, he had had a successful career. Even his father would have to admit that. Though, to be fair, if he hadn't grabbed first, someone else would have grabbed. The thing would have happened without him. He had to admit that. But he had grabbed first and the name known in every home on the face of the earth was Hitler, not any other name. So close, so close . . . A little cold and they died . . . Idiots! And now they wanted to hang him. If he could only get across the border, lie low . . . Until the rest of them got tired of killing Germans. After all, Napoleon came back off Elba. A hundred days. With a little luck he could have stuck . . . Napoleon . . . The name was not to be mentioned. They were going to start worrying about the Russians very soon. The Russians, the Russians . . . The armies had been cut up, they had died by the millions . . . And yet, today they were on the road to Berlin. They were going to need someone to stop the Russians and if he could only lie low for a few months, his name would be mentioned . . . And once he got back, there'd be no more mistakes. With

42

a little luck . . .

The man on the rear seat relaxed against the cushions and a little smile played around the raw mouth.

'I was interviewed by the Washington *Post*,' the booming gentleman was saying, his voice cutting into Peter's reverie. 'Right before I left. And I told them straight up and down – production must not stop.' Peter looked absently at the booming gentleman. He was a tall fat man with a bald head, but somehow he reminded Peter of all the teacher's pets who had ever been in his classes in grammar school – pink, fat face, small, round, pink, satisfied mouth, always impressing everyone with how much he knew and how much in favor he was. Peter closed his eyes and imagined the tall, fat man in an Eton collar with a bow tie and grinned. 'Stop a machine for a day,' the man was saying, 'and industrial obsolescence comes a month nearer. Whether we like it or not we are geared to wartime production.'

'You're so right,' the pretty woman murmured. Peter looked at her closely for the first time. Her clothes were shabby and she had the same wornout, rundown look that the whole country seemed to have, as though the war had rubbed people and things down to the grain, as though the war had kept the whole continent up too many nights, working too hard . . . Teacher's pet was bright and shining, as though he had stepped out of 1941 into a world many years older . . .

'Nobody ever had too many guns. I told them right to their faces.'

'You're so right,' the pretty woman murmured.

'My son was sunk off Alaska . . .' Peter tightened as he recognised the note of boasting in the voice, as though the man were saying he had been elected to an exclusive club. 'My son was sunk off Alaska, and I produced machine tools twenty-four hours a day, seven days a week and I have a right to talk. We got it on our hands, I told them, and we have to face the problem fair and square, what are we going to do with them . . .'

'Yes,' murmured the pretty woman, hoping for dinner, over

the rumble of the wheels.

He would walk slowly, Peter thought, in the evening, after dinner in the big farm kitchen, with the smell of cooking rich and fragrant in the warm kitchen air and his mother red-faced and aproned and his father tall and scrubbed and quiet, smoking his nickel cigar . . . He would walk slowly along the rutted wagon road with Laura beside him in the bright twilight, full of the warm knowledge that he was in no hurry to get any place, that he could leisurely regard the small hills accepting the night, and leisurely listen to the last evening concert of the birds, leisurely scuff his shoes in the light country dust of the road over which armored tread had never passed, which had never known blood. He could tell Laura finally that of all the good things that had happened to him in this savage, ecstatic century, the best had happened in the moment when he had walked toward her on a train platform in Chicago the day after the war was over. He could tell her finally how tired he was, how tired he had been when bone and blood and nerve had collapsed, when no effort had ever seemed possible again, when his body had given up all knowledge of victory or defeat. And when somehow planes had to be flown and guns manned and swift, deadly action taken by that sodden bone and blood and nerve . . . And somehow the action taken because of the feeling deep within him that on other fields and in other skies, wearier and more desperate men were still manning guns for him and flying more dangerous skies . . . And the promise he made to himself that when it was over and he was home, surrounded by care and love, he was never going to hurry again, never knowingly perform a violent act, never even raise his voice except in laughter and song, never argue with anyone about anything . . . He wasn't going back to his job. Nine to five in a bank at a desk was no way to crown a career of bloodshed thirty thousand feet over three continents. Perhaps Laura would be able to suggest something for him to do, something quiet and unhurried and thoughtless . . . But first he was going to do nothing. Just wander around the farm and teach the baby how to spell and listen to his father explain his particular reasons for rotating his crops in

44

his own particular way. Maybe two, three, five months, a year of that, as long as it took to drain off the blood and weariness, as long as it took for his crippled spirit to open the door of its wartime hospital and step out firmly – as long as it took . . .

'The job's just begun,' the booming gentleman was saying. 'Let them ring the bells. It amuses them. But tomorrow morning . . .'

'Yes,' said the pretty woman, eager to agree with everything.

'We've got to face the facts. A businessman faces the facts. What are the facts? The Russians are near Berlin. Right?'

'Yes,' said the woman, 'of course.'

'Berlin. Fine. Unavoidable. The Russians are sitting on Europe . . .'

Peter tried to close his eyes, close his ears, go back to the dear dream of the twilight country road and his wife's hand in his and the dust that had never known blood. But the man's voice tore through and he couldn't help but listen.

'As a businessman I tell you it's an impossible situation.' The man's voice grew louder. 'Intolerable. And the sooner we realise it, the better. The truth is, maybe it's a good thing this war was fought. Dramatises the real problem. Makes the American people see what the real danger is. And what's the answer? Production! Guns and more guns! I don't care what those Communists in Washington say, I say the war has just begun.'

Peter stood up wearily and went over to the booming gentleman. 'Get out of here,' he said as quietly as he could. 'Get out of here and keep quiet or I'll kill you.'

The booming gentleman looked up at him, his face still with surprise. His little red mouth opened twice and closed silently. His pale eyes stared harshly and searchingly at Peter's worn, bitter face. Then he shrugged, stood up, put out his arm for the lady.

'Come,' he said, 'we might as well eat.'

The pretty woman stood up and started hesitantly, frightenedly, toward the door.

'If it weren't for your uniform,' the booming man said loudly, 'I'd have you arrested. Armistice or no Armistice.'

45

'Get out of here,' Peter said.

The booming gentleman turned and walked swiftly after the woman and they disappeared toward the diner. Peter sat down, conscious of every eye in the car on him, regretting that he had found his next years' work placed so soon before him and crying so urgently to be done. Well, he comforted himself, at least I don't have to travel for this one.

The engineer blew his whistle on a ten-mile stretch of clear track because the war was over and as the hoarse, triumphant sound floated back, Peter closed his eyes and tried to think of his wife and child waiting in the noisy station in Chicago. . . .

'Tell her Mr Bloomer wants to see her,' Philip said, holding his hat, standing straight before the elegant, white-handed hotel clerk.

'It's a Mr Bloomer, Miss Gerry,' the hotel clerk said elegantly, looking through Philip's plain, clean face, far across the rich lobby.

Philip heard the famous voice rise and fall in the receiver. 'Who the hell is Mr Bloomer?' the famous sweet voice said.

Philip moved his shoulders uncomfortably in his overcoat. His country-boy ears, sticking out from his rough hair, reddened.

'I heard that,' he said. 'Tell her my name is Philip Bloomer and I wrote a play called *The House of Pain*.'

'It's a Mr Philip Bloomer,' the clerk said languidly, 'and he says he wrote a play called *A House of Pain*.'

'Did he come all the way up here to tell me that?' the deep rich voice boomed in the receiver. 'Tell him that's dandy.'

'Let me talk to her, please.' Philip grabbed the receiver from the clerk's pale hand. 'Hello,' he said, his voice shaking in embarrassment. 'This is Philip Bloomer.'

'How do you do, Mr Bloomer?' the voice said with charm.

'The thing is, Miss Gerry, this play I wrote,' Philip tried to find the subject, the object, the predicate before she hung up, '*The House of Pain*.'

'The clerk said *A House of Pain*, Mr Bloomer.'

'He's wrong,' Philip said.

'He's a very stupid man, that clerk,' the voice said. 'I've told him so many times.'

'I went to Mr Wilkes' office,' Philip said desperately, 'and they said you still had the script.'

'What script?' Miss Gerry asked.

'*The House of Pain*,' Philip cried, sweating. 'When I brought it into Mr Wilkes' office I suggested that you play the leading part and they sent it to you. Now, you see, somebody at the Theatre Guild wants to see the script, and you've had it for two months already, so I thought you mightn't mind letting me have it.'

There was a pause, an intake of breath at the other end of the wire. 'Won't you come up, Mr Bloomer?' Miss Gerry said, her voice chaste but inviting.

'Yes, ma'am,' Philip said.

'1205, sir,' the clerk said, delicately taking the phone from Philip's hands and placing it softly on its pedestal.

In the elevator Philip looked anxiously at his reflection in the mirror, arranged his tie, tried to smooth down his hair. The truth was he looked like a farm boy, a dairy-hand who had perhaps gone to agricultural school for two years. As far as possible he tried to avoid meeting theater people because he knew nobody would believe that anybody who looked like him could write plays.

He got out of the elevator and went down the softly carpeted hall to 1205. There was a sheet of paper stuck in a clip on the metal door. He braced himself and rang the bell.

Miss Adele Gerry opened the door herself. She stood there, tall, dark-haired, perfumed, womanly, in an afternoon dress that showed a square yard of bosom. Her eyes held the same dark fire that had commanded admiring attention on many stages from Brooks Atkinson, from Mantle, from John Mason Brown. She stood there, her hand lightly on the doorknob, her hair swept up simply, her head a little to one side, looking speculatively at Philip Bloomer in the hallway.

'I'm Mr Bloomer,' Philip said.

'Won't you come in?' Her voice was sweet, simple, direct, fitted exactly to the task of allaying the nervousness of farm boys and dairy-hands.

'There's a note for you on the door,' Philip said, glad of one sentence, at least, with which to get inside.

'Oh, thank you,' she said, taking it.

'Probably a letter from some secret admirer,' Philip said, with a smile, suddenly resolved to be gallant, to fight the farm boy, destroy the dairy-hand.

Miss Gerry took the sheet of paper over to the window, scanned it, her eyes close to it near-sightedly, her whole body beautifully intent on the written word.

'It's a menu,' she said, tossing it on a table. 'They have lamb stew tonight.'

Philip closed his eyes for a moment, hoping that when he opened them, Miss Gerry, the room, the hotel would have disappeared.

'Won't you sit down, Mr Bloomer?' Miss Gerry said.

He opened his eyes and marched across the room and sat upright on a little gilt chair. Miss Gerry arranged herself beautifully on a sofa, her hand outstretched along the back, the fingers dangling, the legs girlishly tucked in.

'You know, Mr Bloomer,' Miss Gerry said, her voice charmingly playful, 'you don't look like a playwright at all.'

'I know,' Philip said, gloomily.

'You look so healthy.' She laughed.

'I know.'

'But you *are* a playwright?' She leaned forward intimately, and Philip religiously kept his eyes away from her bosom. This, he suddenly realised, had become the great problem of the interview.

'Oh, yes,' he said, looking steadfastly over her shoulder. 'Yes, indeed. As I told you over the phone, I came up for my play.'

'*The House of Pain.*' She shook her head musingly. 'A lovely title. Such a strange title for such a healthy-looking boy.'

'Yes, ma'am,' Philip said, rigorously holding his head steady, his gaze up.

'It was so good of you to think of me for it,' Miss Gerry said, leaning forward even farther, her eyes liquid and grateful enough to project to the third row, balcony. 'I've practically been in retirement for three years. I thought nobody even remembered Adele Gerry any more.'

49

'Oh, no,' Philip said, gallantly. 'I remembered you.' He saw that this was bad, but was sure that anything else he might add would be worse.

'The Theatre Guild is going to do your play, Mr Bloomer?' Miss Gerry asked fondly.

'Oh, no. I didn't say that. I said somebody I knew up there thought it might not be a bad idea to send it around, and since you'd had the play for two months . . .'

Some of the interest fled from Miss Gerry's deep eyes. 'I haven't a copy of your play, Mr Bloomer. My director, Mr Lawrence Wilkes, has it.' She smiled beautifully at him, although the wrinkles showed clearly then. 'I was interested in seeing you. I like to keep an eye on the new blood of the theater.'

'Thank you,' Philip mumbled, feeling somehow exalted. Miss Gerry beamed at him and he felt his eyes, unable to withstand the full glory of her glance, sinking to her bosom. 'Mr Wilkes,' he said loudly. 'I've seen many of his plays. You were wonderful in his plays. He's a wonderful director.'

'He has his points,' Miss Gerry said coldly. 'But he has limitations. Grave limitations. It is the tragedy of the American theater that there is no man operating in it today who does not suffer from grave limitations.'

'Yes,' Philip said.

'Tell me about your play, Mr Bloomer. Tell me about the part you had in mind for me.' She recrossed her legs comfortably, as though preparing for a long session on the sofa.

'Well,' Philip said, 'it's about a boarding house. A low, dreary, miserable boarding house with bad plumbing and poor devils who can't pay the rent. That sort of thing.'

Miss Gerry said nothing.

'The presiding genius of this boarding house,' Philip went on, 'is a slatternly, tyrannical, scheming, harsh woman. I modeled her on my aunt, who keeps a boarding house.'

'How old is she?' Miss Gerry asked, her voice small and flat.

'Who? My aunt?'

'The woman in the play.'

'Forty-five.' Philip got up and started to stride up and down the room as he talked of his play. 'She's continually snooping around, listening at keyholes, piecing together the tragedies of her boarders from overheard snatches, fighting with her family, fighting with . . . ' He stopped. 'Why, Miss Gerry,' he said. 'Miss Gerry . . . '

She was bent over on the couch and the tears were dropping slowly and bitterly from her eyes.

'That man, 'she wept, 'that man . . . ' She jumped up and swept across to the phone, dialed a number. Unheeded, the tears streamed down through the mascara, eye-shadow, rouge, powder, in dark channels. 'That man,' she wept, 'that man . . . '

Philip backed instinctively against a wall between a table and a chest, his hands spread coldly out behind him. Silently he stood there, like a man awaiting an attack.

'Lawrence!' she cried into the phone. 'I'm glad you were home. There's a young man up here and he's offered me a part in his play.' The tears coursed bitterly down the dark channels on her cheeks. 'Do you know what part it is? I'm going to tell you and then I'm going to throw the young man right the hell out of this hotel!'

Philip cowered against the wall.

'Keep quiet, Lawrence!' Miss Gerry was shouting 'I've listened to your smooth excuses long enough. A woman of forty-five,' she wept, her mouth close to the phone, 'a bitter, slatternly, ugly, hateful boarding-house keeper who listens at keyholes and fights with her family.' Miss Gerry was half bent over in grief now, and she gripped the telephone desperately and clumsily in her two hands. Because her tears were too much for her, she listened and Philip heard a man's voice talking quickly, but soothingly, over the phone.

Finally, disregarding the urgent voice in the receiver, Miss Gerry stood straight. 'Mr Bloomer,' she said, her teeth closing savagely over the name, 'please tell me why you thought of me for this rich and glamorous role.'

Philip braced himself weakly against the wall between the chest and the table. 'You see,' he said, his voice high and boyish and forlorn, 'I saw you in two plays.'

'Shut up, for the love of God!' Miss Gerry called into the phone. Then she looked up and with a cold smile, spoke to Philip. 'What plays, Mr Bloomer?'

'*Sun in the East*,' Philip croaked, 'and *Take the Hindmost*.'

A new and deeper flood of tears formed in her dark eyes. 'Lawrence,' she sobbed into the phone. 'Do you know why he's offering me this part? He saw me in two plays. Your two great successes. He saw me playing a hag of sixty in *Sun in the East* and he saw me playing the mother of a goddamned brood of Irish hoodlums in *Take the Hindmost*. You've ruined me, Lawrence, you've ruined me.'

Philip slipped out of his niche against the wall and walked quickly over to the window and looked out. Twelve stories, his mind registered automatically.

'*Everybody's* seen me in those parts. Everybody! Now, whenever there's a play with a mother, a crone in it, they say, "Call up Adele Gerry." I'm a woman in the full flush of my powers. I should be playing Candida, Hedda, Joan, and I'm everybody's candidate for the hero's old mother! Boarding-house keepers in children's first efforts!'

Philip winced, looking down at Madison Avenue.

'Who did this to me?' Miss Gerry's tones were full, round, tragic. 'Who did it? Who cajoled, pleaded, begged, drove me into those two miserable plays? Lawrence Wilkes! Lawrence Wilkes can claim the credit for ruining the magnificent career of a great actress. The famous Lawrence Wilkes, who fooled me into playing a mother at the age of thirty-three!'

Philip hunched his shoulders as the deep, famous voice crowded the room with sound.

'And now you wonder,' even at the phone, her wide gesture of shoulder and arm was sharp with irony, 'now you wonder why I won't marry you. Send me flowers, send me books, send me tickets to the theater, write me letters telling me you don't care if I go out with other men. From now on I'm going out with the entire garrison of Governor's Island! I'll eat dinner next to you with a different man every night! I hate you, I hate you, Larry, I hate you . . .'

Her sobs finally conquered her. She let the phone drop

52

heedlessly, walked slowly and with pain over to a deep chair and sank into it, damp, bedraggled, undone, like a sorrowing child.

Philip breathed deeply and turned around. 'I'm sorry,' he said hoarsely.

Miss Gerry waved her hand wearily. 'It's not your fault. I've been getting this for three years. You're the agent of events, that's all.'

'Thank you,' Philip said gratefully.

'A young woman like me,' Miss Gerry moaned, looking like a little girl, miserable in the deep chair. 'I'll never get a decent part. Never. Never. Mothers! That man has done me in. Don't ever get mixed up with that man. He's an egotistic maniac. He would crucify his grandmother for a second-act curtain.' She wiped her eyes in a general smear of cosmetics. 'He wants me to marry him.' She laughed horribly.

'I'm so sorry,' Philip said, feeling finally, because that was all he could say, like a farm boy, a dairy-hand. 'I'm so, so sorry.'

'He says go up and get your script,' Miss Gerry said. 'He lives across the street in the Chatham. Just call up from the desk and he'll bring it down.'

'Thank you, Miss Gerry,' Philip said.

'Come here,' she said, the tears departing. He walked slowly over to her and she pulled his head down to her bosom and kissed his forehead and held his ears with her two hands. 'You're a nice, clean, stupid boy,' she said. 'I'm glad to see there's a new crop springing up. Go.'

Philip limped to the door, turned there, meaning to say something, saw Adele Gerry sitting in her chair, looking blankly at the floor, with her face a ruin of sorrow and mascara and age. Philip softly opened the door and softly closed it behind him.

He went across to the street, breathing the cold air deeply, and called Lawrence Wilkes on the phone. Philip recognised Wilkes when he got out of the elevator with a copy of *The House of Pain* under his arm. Wilkes was neatly and beautifully dressed and had a hit running and had just been to a barber, but his face was worn and tortured and weary, like the faces of the people in the newsreels who have just escaped an air-raid, but who do not hope to escape the next.

'Mr Wilkes,' Philip said softly.

Wilkes looked at Philip and smiled and put his head forgivingly and humorously to one side. 'Young man,' he said, 'in the theater you must learn one thing. Never tell an actress what type of part you think she can play.' And he gave Philip *The House of Pain* and turned and went back into the elevator. Philip watched the door close on his well-tailored, tortured back, then sprang out into the street and fled across town to the Theatre Guild.

'I'll go into a nunnery,' Katherine said, holding her books rigidly at her side, as they walked down the street toward Harold's house. 'I'll retire from the world.'

Harold peered uneasily at her through his glasses. 'You can't do that,' he said. 'They won't let you do that.'

'Oh, yes, they will.' Katherine walked stiffly, looking squarely in front of her, wishing that Harold's house was ten blocks farther on. 'I'm a Catholic and I can go into a nunnery.'

'There's no need to do that,' said Harold.

'Do you think I'm pretty?' Katherine asked. 'I'm not looking for compliments. I want to know for a private reason.'

'I think you're pretty,' Harold said. 'I think you're about the prettiest girl in school.'

'Everybody says so,' Katherine said, worrying over the 'about,' but not showing it in her face. 'Of course I don't really think so, but that's what everybody says. You don't seem to think so, either.'

'Oh, yes,' said Harold. 'Oh, yes.'

'From the way you act,' Katherine said.

'It's hard to tell things sometimes,' Harold said, 'by the way people act.'

'I love you,' Katherine said coldly.

Harold took off his glasses and rubbed them nervously with his handkerchief. 'What about Charley Lynch?' he asked, working on his glasses, not looking at Katherine. 'Everybody knows you and Charley Lynch . . . '

'Don't you even like me?' Katherine asked stonily.

'Sure. I like you very much. But Charley Lynch . . . '

'I'm through with him.' Katherine's teeth snapped as she said it. 'I've had enough of him.'

'He's a very nice fellow,' Harold said, putting his glasses on. 'He's the captain of the baseball team and he's the president of the eighth grade and . . . '

'He doesn't interest me,' Katherine said, 'any more.'

They walked silently. Harold subtly increased his speed as they neared his house.

'I have two tickets to Loew's for tonight,' Katherine said.

'Thanks,' said Harold. 'I've got to study.'

'Eleanor Greenberg is giving a party on Saturday night.' Katherine subtly slowed down as she saw Harold's house getting nearer. 'I can bring anyone I want. Would you be interested?'

'My grandmother's,' Harold said. 'We're going to my grandmother's on Saturday. She lives in Doylestown, Pennsylvania. She has seven cows. I go there in the summertime. I know how to milk the cows and they . . . '

'Thursday night,' Katherine said, speaking quickly. 'My mother and father go out on Thursday night to play bridge and they don't come home till one o'clock in the morning. I'm all alone, me and the baby, and the baby sleeps in her own room. I'm all alone,' she said in harsh invitation. 'Would you like to come up and keep me company?'

Harold swallowed unhappily. He felt the blush come up over his collar, surge under his glasses. He coughed loudly, so that if Katherine noticed the blush, she'd think it came from the violence of his coughing.

'Should I slap you on the back?' Katherine asked eagerly.

'No, thank you,' Harold said clearly, his coughing gone.

'Do you want to come up Thursday night?'

'I would like to very much,' Harold said, 'but my mother doesn't let me out at night yet. She says when I'm fifteen . . . '

Katherine's face set in grim lines. 'I saw you in the library at eight o'clock at night, Wednesday.'

'The library's different,' Harold said weakly. 'My mother makes an exception.'

'You could tell her you were going to the library,' Katherine said. 'What's to stop you?'

Harold took a deep, miserable breath. 'Every time I lie

56

my mother knows it,' he said. 'Anyway, you shouldn't lie to your mother.'

Katherine's lip curled with cold amusement. 'You make me laugh,' she said.

They came to the entrance to the apartment house in which Harold lived, and halted.

'In the afternoons,' Katherine said, 'a lot of times nobody's home in the afternoons but me. On your way home from school you could whistle when you pass my window, my room's in front, and I could open the window and whistle back.'

'I'm awful busy,' Harold said, noticing uneasily that Johnson, the doorman, was watching him. 'I've got baseball practice with the Montauk A.C. every afternoon and I got to practice the violin a hour a day and I'm behind in history, there's a lot of chapters I got to read before next month and . . .'

'I'll walk home every afternoon with you,' Katherine said. 'From school. You have to walk home from school, don't you?'

Harold sighed. 'We practice in the school orchestra almost every afternoon.' He stared unhappily at Johnson, who was watching him with the knowing, cynical expression of doormen who see everyone leave and everyone enter and have their own opinions of all entrances and exits. 'We're working on "Poet and Peasant" and it's very hard on the first violins and I never know what time we'll finish and . . .'

'I'll wait for you,' Katherine said, looking straight into his eyes, bitterly, not hiding anything. 'I'll sit at the girls' entrance and I'll wait for you.'

'Sometimes,' said Harold, 'we don't get through till five o'clock.'

'I'll wait for you.'

Harold looked longingly at the doorway to the apartment house, heavy gilt iron and cold glass. 'I'll admit something,' he said. 'I don't like girls very much. I got a lot of other things on my mind.'

'You walk home from school with Elaine,' Katherine said. 'I've seen you.'

'O.K.,' Harold shouted, wishing he could punch the rosy,

57

soft face, the large, coldly accusing blue eyes, the red, quivering lips. 'O.K.!' he shouted, 'I walk home with Elaine! What's it to you? I like to walk home with Elaine! Leave me alone! You've got Charley Lynch. He's a big hero, he pitches for the baseball team. I couldn't even play right field. Leave me alone!'

'I don't want him!' Katherine shouted. 'I'm not interested in Charley Lynch! I hate you!' she cried, 'I hate you! I'm going to retire to a nunnery!'

'Good!' Harold said. 'Very good!' He opened the door of the apartment house. Johnson watched him coldly, unmoving, knowing everything.

'Harold,' Katherine said softly, touching his arm sorrowfully, 'Harold – if you happen to pass my house, whistle "Begin the Beguine." Then I'll know it's you. "Begin the Beguine," Harold . . .'

He shook her hand off, went inside. She watched him walk without looking back at her, open the elevator door, go in, press a button. The door closed finally, and irrevocably behind him. The tears nearly came, but she fought them down. She looked miserably up at the fourth-story window behind which he slept.

She turned and dragged slowly down the block toward her own house. As she reached the corner, her eyes on the pavement before her, a boy spurted out and bumped her.

'Oh, excuse me,' said the boy. She looked up.

'What do you want, Charley?' she asked coldly.

Charley Lynch smiled at her, forcing it. 'Isn't it funny, my bumping into you? Actually bumping into you. I wasn't watching where I was going, I was thinking of something else and . . .'

'Yeah,' said Katherine, starting briskly toward home. 'Yeah.'

'You want to know what I was thinking about?' Charley asked softly, falling in beside her.

'Excuse me,' Katherine said, throwing her head back, all tears gone, looking at a point thirty feet up in the evening sky. 'I'm in a hurry.'

'I was thinking of that night two months ago,' Charley

said quickly. 'That party Norah O'Brien gave. That night I took you home and I kissed your neck. Remember that?'

'No,' she said. She walked at top speed across the street corner, down the row of two-story houses, all alike, with the children playing potsy and skating and leaping out from behind stoops and going, 'A-a-a-a-a-h,' pointing pistols and machine guns at each other. 'Pardon me, I've got to get home and mind the baby; my mother has to go out.'

'You weren't in a hurry with Harold,' Charley said, his eyes hot and dry, as he matched her step for step. 'You walked slow enough with him.'

Katherine looked briefly and witheringly at Charley Lynch. 'I don't know why you think that's your business,' she said. 'It's my own affair.'

'Last month,' Charley said, 'you used to walk home with me.'

'That was last month,' Katherine said loudly.

'What've I done?' Pain sat clearly on Charley Lynch's face, plain over the freckles and the child's nose with the bump on it where a baseball bat had once hit it. 'Please tell me what I've done, Katie.'

'Nothing,' said Katherine, her voice bored and businesslike. 'Absolutely nothing.'

Charley Lynch avoided three small children who were duelling seriously with wooden swords that clanged on the garbage-pail cover shields with which they protected themselves. 'I must have done something,' he said sorrowfully.

'Nothing!' Katherine's tones were clipped and final.

'Put 'em up, Stranger!' a seven-year-old boy said right in front of Charley. He had a pistol and was pointing it at a boy who had another pistol. 'This town ain't big enough for you and me, Stranger,' said the first little boy as Charley went around him, keeping his eyes on Katherine. 'I'll give you twenty-four hours and then come out shooting.'

'Oh, yeah?' said the second little boy with the pistol.

'Do you want to go to the movies tonight?' Charley asked eagerly, rejoining Katherine, safely past the Westerners. 'Cary Grant. Everybody says it's a very funny picture.'

'I would love to go,' said Katherine, 'but I've got to catch up on my reading tonight.'

Charley walked silently among the dueling, wrestling, gun-fighting children. Katherine walked slightly ahead of him, head up, pink and round and rosy-kneed, and Charley looked at the spot on her neck where he had kissed her for the first time and felt his soul drop out of his body.

He laughed suddenly, falsely. Katherine didn't even look at him. 'I was thinking about that feller,' Charley said. 'That Harold. What a name – Harold! He went out for the base-ball team and the coach threw him out the first day. The coach hit three balls at him and they went right through his legs. Then he hit another one at him and it bounced and smacked him right in the nose. You should've seen the look on that Harold's face.' Charley chuckled shrilly. 'We all nearly died laughing. Right square in the nose. You know what all the boys call him? "Four-eyed Oscar." He can't see first base from home plate. "Four-eyed Oscar." Isn't that funny?' Charley asked miserably.

'He's very nice about you,' Katherine turned into the vestibule of her own house. 'He tells me he admires you very much; he thinks you're a nice boy.'

The last trace of the manufactured smile left Charley's face. 'None of the other girls can stand him,' Charley said flatly. 'They laugh at him.'

Katherine smiled secretly, remembering the little girls' conversations in the wardrobes and at recess.

'You think I'm lying!' Charley shouted. 'Just ask.'

Katherine shrugged coolly, her hand on the inner door leading to her house. Charley moved close to her in the vestibule gloom.

'Come to the movies with me,' he whispered. 'Please, Katie, please . . . '

'As I told you, she said, 'I'm busy.'

He put his hand out gropingly, touched hers. 'Katie,' he begged.

She pulled her hand away sharply, opened the door. 'I haven't the time,' she said loudly.

'Please, please . . . ' he whispered.

Katherine shook her head.

Charley spread his arms slowly, lunged for Katherine, hugged her, tried to kiss her. She pulled her head savagely to the side, kicked him sharply in the shins. 'Please . . . 'Charley wept.

'Get out of here!' Katherine slapped his chest with her hands.

Charley backed up. 'You used to let me kiss you,' he said. 'Why not now?'

'I can't be bothered,' Katherine pulled down her dress with sharp, decisive, warning movements.

'I'll tell your mother,' Charley shouted desperately. 'You're going around with a Methodist! With a Protestant!'

Katherine's eyes grew large with fury, her cheeks flooded with blood, her mouth tightened. 'Now get out of here!' she said. 'I'm through with you! I don't want to talk to you. I don't want you to follow me around!'

'I'll walk wherever I goddam please!' Charley yelled.

'I heard what you said,' Katherine said. 'I heard the word you used.'

'I'll follow whoever I goddamn please!' Charley yelled even louder. 'This is a free country.'

'I'll never talk to you as long as I live,' Katherine stamped for emphasis, and her voice rang off the mailboxes and door-knobs of the vestibule. 'You bore me! I'm not interested in you. You're stupid! I don't like you. You're a big idiot! Go home!'

'I'll break his neck for him!' Charley shouted, his eyes clouded, his hands waving wildly in front of Katherine's face. 'I'll show him! A violin player! When I get through with him you won't be so anxious to be seen with him. Do you kiss him?'

'Yes!' Katherine's voice clanged triumphantly. 'I kiss him all the time. And he really knows how to kiss! He doesn't slobber all over a girl like you!'

'Please,' Charley whimpered, 'please . . . ' Hands out gropingly, he went toward Katherine. She drew back her arm coldly, and with all her round, solid, well-nourished, eighty-

61

five pounds, caught him across the face, turned, and fled up the stairs.

'I'll kill him!' Charley roared up the stairwell. 'I'll kill that violinist with my bare hands!'

The door slammed in answer.

'Please tell Mr Harold Pursell,' Charley said soberly to Johnson, the doorman, 'that a certain friend of his is waiting downstairs; he would like to see him, if it's convenient.'

Johnson went up in the elevator and Charley looked with grim satisfaction around the circle of faces of his eight friends, who had come with him to see that everything was carried out in proper order.

Harold stepped out of the elevator, walked toward the boys grouped at the doorway. He peered curiously and short-sightedly at them, as he approached, neat, clean, white-fingered, with his glasses.

'Hello,' Charley stepped out and faced Harold. 'I would like to talk to you in private.'

Harold looked around at the silent ring of faces, drained of pity, brimming with punishment. He sighed, realizing what he was in for.

'All right,' he said, and opened the door, holding it while all the boys filed out.

The walk to the vacant lot in the next block was performed in silence, broken only by the purposeful tramp of Charley Lynch's seconds.

'Take off your glasses,' Charley said when they reached the exact center of the lot.

Harold took off his glasses, looked hesitantly for a place to put them.

'I'll hold them,' Sam Rosenberg, Charley's lieutenant, said politely.

'Thanks,' Harold said, giving him the glasses. He turned and faced Charley, blinking slowly. He put up his hands. 'O.K.' he said.

Charley stood there, breathing deeply, his enemy, blinking, thin-armed, pale, twenty pounds lighter than Charley, before him. A deep wave of exultation rolled through Charley's blood. He put up his hands carefully, stepped in and hit Harold square on the eye with his right hand.

The fight did not take long, although it took longer than Charley had expected. Harold kept punching, advancing into the deadly fire of Charley's fists, the most potent and sharp and brutal in the whole school. Harold's face smeared immediately with blood, and his eye closed, and his shirt tore and the blood soaked in down his clothes. Charley walked in flat-footed, not seeking to dodge or block Harold's weak punches. Charley felt his knuckles smashing against skin and bone and eye, and running with blood, half-delirious with pleasure, as Harold reeled and fell into the cruel, unpitying fists. Even the knuckles on his hands, and the tendons in Charley's fists, carrying the shock of the battle up to his shoulders, seemed to enjoy the pitiless administration of punishment.

From time to time Harold grunted, when Charley took time off from hitting him in the head to hit him, hooking upward from his ankles, in the belly. Except for that, the battle was conducted in complete quiet. The eight friends of Charley watched soberly, professionally, making no comment, finally watching Harold sink to the ground, not unconscious, but too exhausted to move a finger, and lie, spread out, his bloody face pressed harshly, but gratefully, into the dust and rubble of the vacant lot.

Charley stood over the fallen enemy, breathing heavily, his fists tingling joyfully, happy to see the weak, hated, frail figure face down and helpless on the ground, sorry that the pleasure of beating that figure was over. He watched in silence until Harold moved.

'All right,' Harold said, his face still in the dirt. 'That's enough.' He lifted his head, slowly sat up, then, with a trembling hand, pulled himself to his feet. He wavered, his arms out from his sides and shaking uncontrollably, but he held his feet. 'May I have my glasses?' he asked.

Silently, Sam Rosenberg, Charley's lieutenant, gave Harold his glasses. Harold fumblingly, with shaking hands, put them on. Charley watched him, the incongruously undamaged glasses on the damaged face. Suddenly Charley realized that he was crying. He, Charley Lynch, victor in fifty more desperate battles, who had shed no tear since the time he was spanked at the age of four, was weeping uncontrollably, his body shaken with sobs, his eyes hot and smarting. As he wept, he realized that he had been sobbing all through the fight, from the first right-hand to the eye until the final sinking, face-first, of the enemy into the dirt. Charley looked at Harold, eye closed, nose swollen and to one side, hair sweated and muddy, mouth all gore and mud, but the face, the spirit behind it, calm, unmoved. Harold wasn't crying then, Charley knew as he sobbed bitterly, and he wouldn't cry later, and nothing he, Charley Lynch, could ever do would make him cry.

Harold took a deep breath and slowly walked off, without a word.

Charley watched him, the narrow, unheroic, torn and be-draggled back, dragging off. The tears swelled up in a blind flood and Harold disappeared from view behind them.

I STAND BY DEMPSEY

The crowd came out of Madison Square Garden with the sorrowful, meditative air that hangs over it when the fights have been bad. Flanagan pushed Gurske and Flora quickly through the frustrated fans and into a cab. Gurske sat on the folding seat, Flanagan with Flora in the back.

'I want a drink,' he said to her as the cab started. 'I want to forget what I saw tonight.'

'They were not so bad,' Gurske said. 'They were scientific.'

'Not a bloody nose,' Flanagan said. 'Not a single drop of blood. Heavyweights! Heavyweight pansies!'

'As an exhibition of skill,' Gurske said, 'I found it interesting.'

'Joe Louis could've wiped them all up in the short space of two minutes,' Flanagan said.

'Joe Louis is overrated,' Gurske said, leaning across from the little folding seat and tapping Flanagan on the knee. 'He is highly overrated.'

'Yeah,' Flanagan said. 'He is overrated like the S.S. *Texas* is overrated. I saw the Schmeling fight.'

'That German is a old man,' Gurske said.

'When Louis hit him in the belly,' Flora said, 'he cried. Like a baby. Louis' hand went in up to the wrist. I saw with my own eyes.'

'He left his legs in Hamburg,' Gurske said. 'A slight wind woulda knocked him over.'

'That is some slight wind,' said Flanagan, 'that Louis.'

'He's built like a brick privy,' Flora remarked.

'I woulda liked to see Dempsey in there with him.' Gurske rolled his eyes at the thought. 'Dempsey. In his prime. The blood would flow.'

'Louis would make chopmeat outa Dempsey. Who did Dempsey ever beat?' Flanagan wanted to know.

'Listen to that!' Gurske pushed Flora's knee in amazement. 'Dempsey! The Manassa Mauler!'

'Louis is a master boxer,' Flanagan said. 'Also, he punches like he had a baseball bat in both hands. Dempsey! Eugene, you are a goddamn fool.'

'Boys!' Flora said.

'Dempsey was a panther in action. Bobbing and weaving.' Gurske bobbed and weaved and knocked his derby off his small, neat head. 'He carried destruction in either fist.' Gurske bent over for his hat. 'He had the heart of a wounded lion.'

'He certainly would be wounded if he stepped into the ring with Joe Louis.' Flanagan thought this was funny and roared with laughter. He slapped Gurske's face playfully with his huge hand and Gurske's hat fell off.

'You're very funny,' Gurske said, bending over for his hat again. 'You're a very funny man.'

'The trouble with you, Eugene,' Flanagan said, 'is that you don't have no sense of humor.'

'I laugh when something's funny.' Gurske brushed his hat off.

'Am I right?' Flanagan asked Flora. 'Has Eugene got a sense of humor?'

'He is a very serious character, Eugene,' Flora said.

'Go to hell,' Gurske said.

'Hey you.' Flanagan tapped him on the shoulder. 'Don't you talk like that.'

'Aaah,' Gurske said. 'Aaah – '

'You don't know how to argue like a gentleman,' Flanagan said. 'That's what's the matter with you. All little guys're like that.'

'Aaah!'

'A guy is under five foot six, every time he gets in a argument he gets excited. Ain't that so, Flora?'

'Who's excited?' Gurske yelled. 'I am merely stating a fact. Dempsey would lay Louis out like a carpet. That is all I'm saying.'

'You are making too much noise,' Flanagan said. 'Lower your voice.'

'I seen 'em both. With my own eyes!'

'What the hell do you know about fighting, anyway?' Flanagan asked.

'Fighting!' Gurske trembled on his seat. 'The only kind of fighting *you* know about is waiting at the end of a alley with a gun for drunks.'

Flanagan put his hand over Gurske's mouth. With his other hand he held the back of Gurske's neck. 'Shut up, Eugene,' he said. 'I am asking you to shut up.'

'Gurske's eyes rolled for a moment behind the huge hand. Then he relaxed.

Flanagan sighed and released him. 'You are my best friend, Eugene,' he said, 'but sometimes you gotta shut up.'

'A party,' Flora said. 'We go out on a party. Two gorillas. A little gorilla and a big gorilla.'

They rolled downtown in silence. They brightened, however, when they got to Savage's Café and had two Old-Fashioneds each. The five-piece college-boy band played fast numbers and the Old-Fashioneds warmed the blood and friends gathered around the table. Flanagan stretched out his hand and patted Gurske amiably on the head.

'All right,' he said. 'All right, Eugene. We're friends. You and me, we are lifelong comrades.'

'All right,' Gurske said reluctantly. 'This is a party.'

Everybody drank because it was a party, and Flora said, 'Now, boys, you see how foolish it was — over two guys you never even met to talk to?'

'It was a question of attitude,' Gurske said. 'Just because he's a big slob with meat axes for hands he takes a superior attitude.'

'All I said was Louis was a master boxer.' Flanagan opened his collar.

'That's all he said!'

'Dempsey was a slugger. That's all — a slugger. Look what that big ox from South America did to him. That Firpo.

Dempsey had to be put on his feet by newspapermen. No newspaper man has to stand Joe Louis on his feet.'

'That's all he said,' Gurske repeated. 'That's all he said. My God!'

'Boy,' Flora pleaded, 'it's history. Have a good time.'

Flanagan toyed with his glass. 'That Eugene,' he said. 'You say one thing, he says another. Automatic. The whole world agrees there never was nothing like Joe Louis, he brings up Dempsey.'

'The whole world!' Gurske said. 'Flanagan, the whole world!'

'I want to dance,' Flora said.

'Sit down,' Flanagan said. 'I want to talk with my friend, Eugene Gurske.'

'Stick to the facts,' Gurske said. 'That's all I ask, stick to the facts.'

'A small man can't get along in human society,' Flanagan said to the company at the table. 'He can't agree with no one. He should live in a cage.'

'That's right,' Gurske said. 'Make it personal. You can't win by reason, use insults. Typical.'

'I would give Dempsey two rounds. Two,' Flanagan said. 'There! As far as I am concerned the argument is over. I want a drink.'

'Let me tell you something,' Gurske said loudly. 'Louis wouldn't – '

'The discussion is closed.'

'Who says it's closed? In Shelby, Montana, when Dempsey – '

'I ain't interested.'

'He met 'em all and beat 'em all – '

'Listen, Eugene,' Flanagan said seriously. 'I don't want to hear no more. I want to listen to the music.'

Gurske jumped up from his chair in a rage. 'I'm goin' to talk, see, and you're not going to stop me, see, and – '

'Eugene,' Flanagan said. Slowly he lifted his hand, palm open.

'I – ' Gurske watched the big red hand, with the heavy gold

68

rings on the fingers, waggle back and forth. His lips quivered. He stooped suddenly and picked up his derby and rushed out of the room, the laughter of the guests at the table ringing in his ears.

'He'll be back,' Flanagan said. 'He's excitable, Eugene. Like a little rooster. He has to go to be toned down now and then. Now, Flora. Let's dance.'

They danced pleasantly for a half-hour, taking time out for another Old-Fashioned between numbers. They were on the dance floor when Gurske appeared in the doorway with a large soda bottle in each hand.

'Flanagan!' Gurske shouted from the doorway. 'I'm looking for Vincent Flanagan!'

'My God!' Flora shrieked. 'He'll kill somebody!'

'Flanagan,' Gurske repeated. 'Come on out of that crowd. Step out here.'

Flora pulled at Flanagan as the dancers melted to both sides. 'Vinnie,' she cried, 'there's a back door.'

'Give me a ginger-ale bottle,' Flanagan said, taking a step toward Gurske. 'Somebody put a ginger-ale bottle in my hand.'

'Don't come no nearer, Flanagan! This is one argument you won't win with yer lousy big hands.'

'Where is that ginger-ale bottle?' Flanagan asked, advancing on Gurske step by step, keeping Gurske's eyes fixed with his.

'I warn you, Flanagan!'

Gurske threw one of the bottles. Flanagan ducked and it smashed against the back wall.

'You are going to regret this,' Flanagan said.

Gurske lifted the other bottle nervously. Flanagan took another step, and then another.

'Oh, my God!' Gurske cried, and threw the bottle at Flanagan's head and turned tail and ran.

Flanagan caught the bottle in mid-flight, took careful aim with it, and let it go across the dance floor. It hit Gurske at the ankle and he went sailing over a table like a duckpin caught all alone on a bowling alley. Flanagan was on him and had him by the collar immediately. He lifted Gurske into the air with one hand and held him there.

'Gurske,' he said. 'You cockeyed Gurske. The hundred-and-thirty-pound Napoleon.'

'Don't kill him!' Flora running over to them distractedly. 'For God's sake, don't kill him, Vinnie!'

For a moment Flanagan looked at Gurske hanging limply from his hand. Then he turned to the other guests. 'Ladies and gentlemen,' he said, 'no damage has occurred.'

'I missed,' Gurske said bitterly. 'I ought to wear glasses.'

'Let everybody dance,' Flanagan announced. 'I apologize for my friend. I guarantee he won't cause no more trouble.'

The orchestra struck up 'The Dipsy Doodle' and the guests swung back with animation into their dancing.

Flanagan carried Gurske to their table and set him down. 'All right,' he said. 'We will finish our discussion. Once and for all.'

'Aaah!' Gurske said, but without spirit.

'Eugene.' Flanagan said, 'come here.'

Gurske sidled up toward Flanagan, who was sitting with his feet out from the table, his legs spread comfortably apart.

'What about those prizefighters we mentioned some time ago?'

'Dempsey,' Gurske said hoarsely. 'I stand by Dempsey.'

Flanagan laid his hand on Gurske's arm and pulled. Gurske fell face downward, seat up, over Flanagan's knees.

'The old woodshed,' Flanagan said. He began to spank Gurske with wide, deliberate strokes. The orchestra stopped playing after a moment and the smacks resounded in the silent room.

'Oh!' Gurske said at the seventh stroke.

'Oh!' the roomful of people answered in a single hushed tone.

At the ninth stroke the drummer of the band took up the beat and from then on the bass drum sounded simultaneously with the hard, unrelenting hand.

'Well,' Flanagan said on the twenty-fifth stroke. 'Well, Mr Gurske?'

70

'I stand by Dempsey!'

'O.K.' Flanagan said, and continued with the spanking.

After stroke thirty-two Gurske called tearfully, 'All right. That's all, Flanagan.'

Flanagan lifted Eugene to his feet. 'I am glad that matter is settled. Now sit down and have a drink.'

The guests applauded and the orchestra struck up and the dancing began again. Flanagan and Flora and Gurske sat at their table drinking Old Fashioneds.

'The drinks are on me,' Flanagan said. 'Drink hearty. Who do you stand by, Eugene?'

'I stand by Louis,' Gurske said.

'What round would he win in?'

'In the second round,' Gurske said. The tears streamed down his face, and he sipped his Old-Fashioned. 'He would win in the second round.'

'My friend Eugene,' Flanagan said.

STOP PUSHING, ROCKY

Mr Gensel carefully wrapped six feet of adhesive tape around Joey Garr's famous right hand. Joey sat on the edge of the rubbing table, swinging his legs, watching his manager moodily.

'Delicate,' Mr Gensel said, working thoughtfully. 'Remember, delicate is the keyword.'

'Yeah,' Joey said. He belched.

Mr Gensel frowned and stopped winding the tape. 'Joey,' he said, 'how many times I got to tell you, please, for my sake, don't eat in diners.'

'Yeah,' Joey said.

'There is a limit to everything, Joey,' Mr Gensel said. 'Thrift can be carried too far, Joey. You're not a poor man. You got as much money in the bank as a Hollywood actress, why do you have to eat thirty-five-cent blueplates?'

'Please do not talk so much.' Joey stuck out his left hand.

Mr Gensel turned his attention to the famous left hand. 'Ulcers,' he complained. 'I will have a fighter with ulcers. A wonderful prospect. He has to eat garbage. Garbage and ketchup. The coming welter-weight champion. Dynamite in either fist. But he belches forty times a day. My God, Joey.'

Joey sat impassively on the floor and squinted at his neatly slicked hair in the mirror. Mr Gensel sighed and moved his bridge restlessly around in his mouth and finished his job.

'Allow me, some day,' he said, 'to buy you a meal. A dollar-fifty meal. To give you the taste.'

'Save yer money, Mr Gensel,' Joey said, 'for your old age.'

The door opened and McAlmon came in, flanked on either side by two tall, broad men with flat faces and scarred lips curled in amiable grins.

'I am glad to see you boys,' McAlmon said, coming up and

patting Joey on the back. 'How is my little Joey tonight?'

'Yeah,' Joey said, lying down on the rubbing table and closing his eyes.

'He belches,' Mr Gensel said. 'I never saw a fighter belched so much as Joey in my whole life. Not in thirty-five years in the game. How is your boy?'

'Rocky is fine,' McAlmon said. 'He wanted to come in here with me. He wanted to make sure that Joey understood.'

'I understand,' Joey said irritably. 'I understand fine. That Rocky. The one thing he is afraid of maybe someday somebody will hit him. A prize fighter.'

'You can't blame him,' McAlmon said reasonably. 'After all, he knows, if Joey wants he can put him down until the day after Thanksgiving.'

'With one hand,' Joey said grimly. 'That is some fighter, that Rocky.'

'He got nothing to worry about,' Mr Gensel said smoothly. 'Everything is absolutely clear in everybody's mind. Clear like crystal. We carry him the whole ten rounds.'

'Lissen, Joey,' McAlmon leaned on the rubbing table right over Joey's upturned face, 'let him look good. He has a following in Philadelphia.'

'I will make him look wonderful,' Joey said wearily. 'I will make him look like the British navy. The one thing that worries me all the time is maybe Rocky will lose his following in Philadelphia.'

McAlmon spoke very coldly. 'I don't like your tone of voice, Joey,' he said.

'Yeah.' Joey turned over on his belly.

'Just in case,' McAlmon said in crisp tones, 'just in case any party forgets their agreement, let me introduce you to Mr Pike and Mr Petroskas.'

The two tall broad men smiled very widely.

Joey sat up slowly and looked at them.

'They will be sitting in the audience,' McAlmon said. 'Watching proceedings with interest.'

The two men smiled from ear to ear, the flat noses flattening even deeper into their faces.

'They got guns, Mr Gensel,' Joey said. 'Under their lousy armpits.'

'It is just a precaution,' McAlmon said. 'I know everything will go along smooth. But we got money invested.'

'Lissen, you dumb Philadelphia hick,' Joey began.

'That isn't the way to talk, Joey,' Mr Gensel said nervously.

'I got money invested, too,' Joey yelled. 'I got one thousand dollars down even money that that lousy Rocky stays ten rounds with me. You don't need your gorillas. I am only hoping Rocky don't collapse from fright before the tenth round.'

'Is that the truth?' McAlmon asked Mr Gensel.

'I put the bet down through my own brother-in-law,' Mr Gensel said. 'I swear to God.'

'What do you think, McAlmon?' Joey shouted, 'I throw away thousand-dollar bills? I'm a business man.'

'Take my word for it,' Mr Gensel said. 'Joey is a business man.'

'All right, all right.' McAlmon put out both his hands placatingly. 'There is no harm done in straightening matters out complete beforehand, is there? Now nobody is in the dark about anything. That is the way I like to operate.' He turned to Pike and Petroskas. 'O.K., boys, just sit in your seats and have a good time.'

'Why do these two bums have to be there?' Joey demanded.

'Do you mind if they enjoy themselves?' McAlmon asked with cold sarcasm. 'It's going to damage you if they have a good time?'

'That's all right,' Mr Gensel said soothingly. 'We don't object. Let the boys have a good time.'

'Only get them out of here,' Joey said loudly. 'I don't like people with guns under their armpits in my room.'

'Come on, boys,' McAlmon said, opening the door. Both men smiled pleasantly and started out. Petroskas stopped and turned around. 'May the best man win,' he said, and nodded soberly twice and left, closing the door behind him.

Joey looked at Mr Gensel and shook his head. 'McAlmon's friends,' he said. 'Philadelphia boys.'

The door swung open and an usher chanted 'Joey Garr. Joey Garr is on next.' Joey spat into his bandaged hands and started up the steps with Mr Gensel.

When the fight started, Rocky dove immediately into a clinch. Under the thick bush of hair all over his chest and shoulders he was sweating profusely

'Lissen, Joey,' he whispered nervously into Joey's ear, hanging on tightly to his elbows, 'you remember the agreement? You remember, don't yuh, Joey?'

'Yeah,' Joey said. 'Let go of my arm. What're you trying to do, pull it off?'

'Excuse me, Joey,' Rocky said, breaking and giving Joey two to the ribs.

As the fight progressed, with the customers yelling loud approval of the footwork, the deft exchanges, the murderous finishers, that missed by a hair, Rocky gained in confidence. By the fourth round he was standing up bravely, exposing his chin, moving in and out with his fists brisk and showy. His friends in the crowd screamed with pleasure and a loud voice called out, 'Kill the big bum, Rocky! Oh, you Rocky!' Rocky breathed deeply and let a fast one go to Joey's ear. Joey's head shook a little and a look of mild surprise came over his face. 'Wipe him out!' the voice thundered from among Rocky's following. Rocky set himself flat on his feet and whistled another across to Joey's ear as the bell rang. He strutted back to his corner smiling confidently at his friends in the arena.

Mr Gensel bent and worked over Joey. 'Lissen, Joey, he whispered, 'he is pushing you. Tell him to stop pushing you. They will give him the fight if he don't stop pushing you.'

'Aaah,' Joey said, 'it's nothing. For the crowd. His pals. A little excitement. Makes it look good. Don't worry, Mr Gensel.'

'Please tell him to stop pushing you,' Mr Gensel pleaded. 'For my sake, Joey. He is supposed to go ten rounds with us but we are supposed to win. We can't afford to lose to Rocky Pidgeon, Joey.'

In the fifth round Rocky kept up his charging attack, keeping both hands going, weaving, aggressive, shoving Joey back and forth across the ring, while the home-town crowd stood in its seats and shouted hoarse support. Joey kept him nicely bottled up, back-pedaling, catching punches on his gloves, sliding with the blows, occasionally jabbing sharply to Rocky's chest. In a corner, with Joey against the ropes, Rocky swung from behind his back with a right hand, grunting deeply as it landed on Joey's side.

Joey clinched, feeling the sting. 'Say, Rocky,' he whispered politely, 'stop pushing.'

'Oh,' Rocky grunted, as though he'd just remembered, and backed off. They sparred delicately for thirty seconds, Joey still on the ropes.

'Come on, Rocky,' the voice shouted. 'Finish him. You got the bum going! Oh, you Rocky!'

A light came into Rocky's eyes and he would up and let one go. It caught Joey on the side of the head as the bell rang. Joey leaned a little wearily against the ropes, scowling thoughtfully at Rocky as Rocky strode lightly across to his corner amid wild applause. Joey went and sat down.

'How's it going? he asked Mr Gensel.

'You lost that round,' Mr Gensel said swiftly and nervously. 'For God's sake, Joey, tell him to stop pushing. You'll lose the fight. If you lose to Rocky Pidgeon you will have to fight on the team with the boys from the Hebrew Orphan Asylum. Why don't you tell him to stop pushing?'

'I did,' Joey snapped. 'He's all hopped up. His friends keep yelling what a great guy he is, so he believes it. He hits me in the ear once more I will take him out in the alley after the fight and I will beat the pants off him.'

'Just tell him to take it easy,' Mr Gensel said, worriedly. 'Remind him we are carrying him. Just remind him.'

'That dumb Rocky,' Joey said. 'You got to reason with him, you got a job on your hands.'

The gong rang and the two men sprang out at each other. The light of battle was still in Rocky's eye and he came out swinging violently. Joey tied him up tight and talked earnestly to him. 'Lissen, Rocky, enough is enough. Stop being a hero, please. Everybody thinks you're wonderful. All right. Let it go at that. Stop pushing, Rocky. There is money invested here. What are you, crazy? Say, Rocky, do you know what I'm talking about?'

'Sure,' Rocky grunted. 'I'm just putting on a good show. You got to put on a good show, don't you?'

'Yeah,' Joey said, as the referee finally pulled them apart.

They danced for two minutes after that, but right before the end of the round, from in close, Rocky unleashed a murderous uppercut that sent the blood squirting in all directions from Joey's nose. Rocky wheeled jauntily as the bell rang and shook his hands gaily at his screaming friends. Joey looked after him and spat a long stream of blood at his retreating, swaggering back.

Mr Gensel rushed anxiously out and led Joey back to his corner.

'Why didn't you tell him to stop pushing, Joey?' he asked. 'Why don't you do like I say?'

'I told him,' Joey said, bitterly. 'Look, I got a bloody nose. I got to come to Philadelphia to get a bloody nose. That bastid, Rocky.'

'Make sure to tell him to stop pushing,' Mr Gensel said, working swiftly over the nose. 'You got to win from here on, Joey. No mistake now.'

'I got to come to Starlight Park, in the city of Philadelphia,' Joey marveled, 'to get a bloody nose from Rocky Pidgeon. Holy Jesus God!'

'Joey,' Mr Gensel implored, 'will you remember what I told you? Tell him to stop . . .'

The bell rang and the two men leapt at each other as the crowd took up its roaring from where it had left off. The loud voice had settled into a constant, inspiriting chant of 'Oh, Rocky, oh, you Rocky!' over and over again.

Joey grabbed Rocky grimly. 'Lissen, you bum,' he whispered harshly. 'I ask you to stop pushing. I will take you out later and knock all your teeth out. I warn you.'

And he rapped Rocky smartly twice across the ear to impress him.

For the next minute Rocky kept a respectful distance and

Joey piled up points rapidly. Suddenly half the arena took up the chant, 'Oh, Rocky, oh, you Rocky!' On fire with this admiration, Rocky took a deep breath and let sail a roundhouse right. It caught Joey squarely on the injured nose. Once more the blood spurted. Joey shook his head to clear it and took a step toward Rocky, who was charging in wildly. Coldly Joey hooked with his left, like a spring uncoiling, and crossed with his right as Rocky sagged with glass in his eyes. Rocky went fourteen feet across the ring and landed face down. For a split second a smile of satisfaction crossed Joey's face. Then he remembered. He swallowed drily as the roar of the crowd exploded in his ears. He looked at his corner. Mr Gensel was just turning around to sit with his back to the ring and his head in his hands. He looked at Rocky's corner. McAlmon was jumping up and down, beating his hat with both fists in agony, screaming, 'Rocky! Get up. Rocky! Get up or I'll fill you full of lead! Rocky, do you hear me?'

Behind McAlmon, Joey saw Pike and Petraskas, standing in their seats, amiable smiles on their faces, watching him interestedly, their hands under their armpits.

'Rocky!' Joey whispered hoarsely as the referee counted five, 'Good old Rocky. Get up, Rocky! For God's sake. Please get up! Please . . . please.' He remembered the thousand dollars and tears filled his eyes. 'Rocky,' he sobbed, half-bending to his knees, in the corner of the ring, as the referee reached seven, 'for the love of God . . . '

Rocky turned over, got to one knee.

Joey closed his eyes to spare himself. When he opened them again, there was Rocky, standing, weaving unsteadily, before him. A breath, a prayer, escaped Joey's lips as he jumped across the ring, swinging dramatically. He curled his arm viciously around the back of Rocky's neck. Even at that Rocky started to go again. Joey grabbed him under the armpits and made violent movements with his arms as though he were trying desperately to release them.

'Hold on, Rocky!' he whispered hoarselw, supporting the stricken fighter. 'Just keep your knees stiff. You all right? Hey, Rocky, you all right? Hey, Rocky, answer me! Please,

78

Rocky, say something!'

But Rocky said nothing. He just leaned against Joey with the glaze in his eyes, his arms hanging limply at his side, while Joey conducted the fight by himself.

When the bell rang, Joey held Rocky up until McAlmon could come out and drag him back to his corner. The referee eyed Joey narrowly as Joey went over to his own corner.

'A nice, interesting bout,' the referee said. 'Yes, sirree.'

'Yeah,' Joey said, sinking on to his stool. 'Hey, Mr Gensel,' he called. Mr Gensel turned his face back to the ring for the first time since the middle of the round. Like an old man, he climbed the steps and haphazardly worked on his fighter.

'Explain to me,' he said in a flat voice, 'what you were thinking of.'

'That Rocky,' Joey said wearily. 'He got the brains of a ice-man's horse. He keeps pushing and pushing. I musta lost a quart of blood through the nose. I hit him to teach him a little respect.'

'Yes,' Mr Gensel said. 'That was fine. We were nearly buried in Philadelphia.'

'I didn't hit him hard,' Joey protested. 'It was strictly a medium punch. He got a chin like a movie star. Like Myrna Loy. He shouldn't oughta be in this business. He should wait on customers in a store. In a dairy. Butter and eggs.'

'Please do me a favor,' Mr Gensel said. 'Kindly hold him up for the next three rounds. Treat him with care. I am going to sit in the dressing room.'

And Mr Gensel left as Joey charged out and pounded Rocky's fluttering elbows severely.

Fifteen minutes later, Joey came down to him in the dressing room and lay wearily down on the rubbing table.

'So?' Mr Geisel asked, not lifting his head.

'So we won,' Joey said hoarsely. 'I had to carry him like a baby for nine whole minutes. Like a eight-month-old baby girl. That Rocky. Hit him once, he is no good for three years. I never worked so hard in my whole life, not even when I poured rubber in Akron, Ohio.'

'Did anybody catch on?' Mr Gensel asked.

'Thank God we're in Philadelphia,' Joey said. 'They ain't caught on the war's over yet. They are still standing up there yelling, Rocky! Oh, you Rocky!' because he was so goddamn brave and stood in there fighting. My God! Every ten seconds I had to kick him in the knee to straighten it out so he'd keep standing!'

Mr Gensel sighed. 'Well, we made a lot of money.'

'Yeah,' Joey said without joy.

'I'll treat you to a dollar-fifty dinner, Joey.'

'Naah,' Joey said, flattening out on the rubbing table. 'I just want to stay here and rest, I want to lay here and rest for a long time.'

THE DEPUTY SHERIFF

Macomber sat in the sheriff's swivel chair, his feet in the waste-basket because he was too fat to lift them to the desk. He sat there looking across at the poster on the opposite wall that said, 'Wanted, for Murder, Walter Cooper, Reward Four Hundred Dollars.' He sometimes sat for seven days on end looking at the spot that said 'Four Hundred Dollars,' going out only for meals and ten hours' sleep a night.

Macomber was the third deputy sheriff and he took care of the office because he didn't like to go home to his wife. In the afternoon the second deputy sheriff came in, too, and sat tilted against the wall, also looking at the spot that said, 'Four Hundred Dollars.'

'I read in the newspapers,' Macomber said, feeling the sweat roll deliberately down his neck into his shirt, 'that New Mexico has the healthiest climate in the world. Look at me sweat. Do you call that healthy?'

'You're too gaddamn fat,' the second deputy sheriff said, never taking his eyes off the 'Four Hundred Dollars.' 'What do you expect?'

'You could fry eggs,' Macomber said, looking for an instant at the street blazing outside his window.'I need a vacation. You need a vacation. Everybody needs a vacation.' He shifted his gun wearily, where it dug into the fat. 'Why can't Walter Cooper walk in here this minute? Why can't he?' he asked.

The telephone rang. Macomber picked it up. He listened, said, 'Yes, no, the sheriff's taking a nap. I'll tell him, goodbye.'

He put the telephone down slowly, thought in his eyes. 'That was Los Angeles,' he said. 'They caught Brisbane. They got him in the jail there.'

'He'll get fifteen years,' the second deputy said. 'His accomplice got fifteen years. They can sing to each other.'

'That's my case,' Macomber said, slowly, putting on his hat. 'I was the first one to look at the boxcar after they burst into it.' He turned at the door. 'Somebody's got to go bring Brisbane back from Los Angeles. I'm the man, wouldn't you say?'

'You're the man,' the second deputy said. 'That's a nice trip. Hollywood. There is nothing wrong with the girls in Hollywood.' He nodded his head dreamily. 'I wouldn't mind shaking a hip in that city.'

Macomber walked slowly toward the sheriff's house, smiling a little to himself, despite the heat, as he thought of Hollywood. He walked briskly, his two hundred and forty pounds purposeful and alert.

'Oh, for Christ's sake,' the sheriff said when he told him about Brisbane, 'what the hell turns up in Los Angeles.' The sheriff was sleepy and annoyed, sitting on the edge of the sofa on which he'd been lying without shoes, his pants open for the first three buttons, after lunch. 'We got a conviction out of that, already.'

'Brisbane is a known criminal,' Macomber said. 'He committed entry.'

'So he committed entry,' the sheriff said. 'Into a boxcar. He took two overcoats and a pair of socks and I have to send a man to Los Angeles for him! If you asked them for a murderer you'd never get him out of Los Angeles in twenty years! Why did you have to wake me up?' he asked Macomber testily.

'Los Angeles asked me to have you call back as soon as possible,' Macomber said smoothly. 'They want to know what to do with him. They want to get rid of him. He cries all day, they told me, at the top of his voice. He's got a whole cellblock yelling their heads off in Los Angeles, they told me.'

'I need a man like that here,' the sheriff said. 'I need him very bad.'

But he put his shoes on and buttoned his pants and started back to the office with Macomber.

'Do you mind going to Los Angeles?' the sheriff asked Macomber.

Macomber shrugged. 'Somebody's got to do it.'

'Good old Macomber, 'the sheriff said sarcastically. 'The backbone of the force. Ever loyal.'

'I know the case,' Macomber said. 'Inside out.'

The sheriff looked at him over his shoulder. 'There are so many girls there, I read, that even a fat man ought to be able to do business. Taking your wife, Macomber?' He jabbed with his thumb into the fat over the ribs, and laughed.

'Somebody's got to go. I admit,' Macomber said earnestly, 'it would be nice to see Hollywood. I've read about it.'

When they got into the office the second deputy got up out of the swivel chair, and the sheriff dropped into it, unbuttoning the top three buttons of his pants. The sheriff opened a drawer and took out a ledger, panting from the heat. 'Why is it,' the sheriff wanted to know, 'that anybody lives in a place like this?' He looked with annoyance at the opened ledger. 'We have not got a penny,' the sheriff said, 'not a stinking penny. That trip to Needles after Bucher cleaned out the fund. We don't get another appropriation for two months. This is a beautiful county. Catch one crook and you got to go out of business for the season. So what are you looking at me like that for, Macomber?'

'It wouldn't cost more than ninety dollars to send a man to Los Angeles.' Macomber sat down gently on a small chair.

'You got ninety dollars?' the sheriff asked.

'This got nothing to do with me,' Macomber said. 'Only it's a known criminal.'

'Maybe,' the second deputy said, 'you could get Los Angeles to hold on to him for two months.'

'I got brain workers in this office,' the sheriff said. 'Regular brain workers.' But he turned to the phone and said, 'Get me the police headquarters at Los Angeles.'

'Swanson is the name of the man who is handling the matter,' Macomber said. 'He's waiting for your call.'

'Ask them to catch a murderer in Los Angeles,' the sheriff said bitterly, 'and see what you get . . . They're wonderful on people who break into boxcars.'

While the sheriff was waiting for the call to be put through, Macomber turned ponderously, the seat of his pants sticking to the yellow varnish of the chair, and looked out at the deserted street, white with sunlight, the tar boiling up in little black bubbles out in the road from the heat. For a moment, deep under the fat, he couldn't bear Gatlin, New Mexico. A suburb of the desert, a fine place for people with tuberculosis. For twelve years he'd been there, going to the movies twice a week, listening to his wife talk. The fat man. Before you died in Gatlin, New Mexico, you got fat. Twelve years, he thought, looking out on a street that was empty except on Saturday night. He could see himself stepping out of a barber shop in Hollywood, walking lightly to a bar with a blonde girl, thin in the waist, drinking a beer or two, talking and laughing in the middle of a million other people talking and laughing. Greta Garbo walked the streets there, and Carole Lombard, and Alice Faye. 'Sarah,' he would say to his wife, 'I have to go to Los Angeles. On State business. I will not be back for a week.'

'Well . . . ?' the sheriff was calling into the phone. '*Well?* Where is Los Angeles?'

Ninety dollars, ninety lousy dollars . . . He turned away from looking at the street. He put his hands on his knees and was surprised to see them shake as he heard the sheriff say, 'Hello, is this Swanson?'

He couldn't sit still and listen to the sheriff talk over the phone, so he got up and walked slowly through the back room to the lavatory. He went in, closed the door, and looked carefully at his face in the mirror. That's what his face looked like, that's what the twelve years, listening to his wife talk, had done. Without expression he went back to the office.

'All right,' the sheriff was saying, 'you don't have to keep him for two months. I know you're crowded. I know it's against the constitution. I know, I said, for Christ's sake. It was just a suggestion. I'm sorry he's crying. Is it my fault he's crying? Maybe you'd cry, too, if you were going to jail for fifteen years. Stop yelling, for Christ's sake, this call is costing the county of Gatlin a million dollars. I'll call you back. All right, by six o'clock. All right, I said. All right.'

The sheriff put the telephone down. For a moment he sat wearily, looking at the open top of his pants. He sighed, buttoned his pants. 'That is some city,' he said, 'Los Angeles.' He shook his head. 'I got a good mind to say the hell with it. Why should I run myself into an early grave for a man who broke into a boxcar? Who can tell me?'

'He's a known criminal,' Macomber said. 'We got a whole case.' His voice was smooth but he felt the eager tremor deep under it. 'Justice is justice.'

The sheriff looked at him bitterly. 'The voice of conscience. The sheriff's white light, Macomber.'

Macomber shrugged. 'What's it to me? I just like to see a case closed.'

The sheriff turned back to the telephone. 'Get me the county treasurer's office,' he said. He sat there, waiting, looking at Macomber, with the receiver against his ear. Macomber walked over to the door and looked out across the street. He saw his wife sitting at the window of their house up the street, her fat elbows crossed, with sweat dripping off them. He looked the other way.

He heard the sheriff's voice, as though distant and indistinct, talking to the county treasurer. He heard the county treasurer's voice rise in anger through the phone, mechanical and shrill. 'Everybody spends money,' the county treasurer screamed. 'Nobody brings in money, but everybody spends money. I'll be lucky to have my own salary left over at the end of the month and you want ninety dollars to go joy-riding to Los Angeles to get a man who stole nine dollars' worth of second-hand goods. The hell with you! I said the hell with you!'

Macomber put his hands in his pockets so that nobody could see how tense they were as he heard the receiver slam on the other end of the wire. Coldly he watched the sheriff put the phone gently down.

'Macomber,' the sheriff said, feeling his deputy's eyes on him, hard and accusing, 'I'm afraid Joan Crawford will have to get along without you, this year.'

'They will hang crepe on the studios when they hear about this,' the second deputy said.

'I don't care for myself,' Macomber said evenly, 'but it will sound awfully funny to people if they find out that the sheriff's office let a known criminal go free after he was caught.'

The sheriff stood up abruptly. 'What do you want me to do?' he asked with violence. 'Tell me what the hell more you want me to do? Can I create the ninety dollars? Talk to the State of New Mexico!'

Macomber shrugged. 'It's not my business,' he said. 'Only I think we can't let criminals laugh at New Mexican justice.'

'All right,' the sheriff shouted. 'Do something. Go do something! I don't have to call back until six o'clock! You got three hours to see justice done. My hands are washed.' He sat down and opened the top three buttons of his pants and put his feet on the desk. 'If it means so much to you,' he said, as Macomber started through the door, '"arrange it yourself.'

Macomber passed his house on the way to the district attorney's office. His wife was still sitting at the window with the sweat dripping off her. She looked at her husband out of her dry eyes, and he looked at her as he walked thoughtfully past. No smile lit her face or his, no word was passed. For a moment they looked at each other with the arid recognition of twelve years. Then Macomber walked deliberately on, feeling the heat rising through his shoes, tiring his legs right up to his hips.

In Hollywood he would walk firmly and briskly, not like a fat man, over the clean pavements, ringing to the sharp attractive clicks of high heels all around him. For ten steps he closed his eyes as he turned into the main street of Gatlin, New Mexico.

He went into the huge Greek building that the W.P.A. had built for the County of Gatlin. As he passed down the quiet halls, rich with marble, cool, even in the mid-afternoon, he said, looking harshly around him, 'Ninety dollars – ninety lousy dollars.'

In front of the door that said 'Office of the District

Attorney' he stopped. He stood there for a moment, feeling nervousness rise and fall in him like a wave. His hand sweated on the doorknob when he opened the door. He went in casually, carefully appearing like a man carrying out impersonal government business.

The door to the private office was open a little and he could see the district attorney yelling, 'For God's sake, Carol, have a heart! Do I look like a man who is made of money? Answer me, do I?'

'All I want,' the district attorney's wife said stubbornly, 'is a little vacation. Three weeks, that's all. I can't stand the heat here. I'll lie down and die if I have to stay here another week. Do you want me to lie down and die? You make me live in this oasis, do I have to die here, too?' She started to cry, shaking her careful blonde hair.

'All right,' the district attorney said. 'All right, Carol. Go ahead. Go home and pack. Stop crying. For the love of God, stop crying!'

She went over and kissed the district attorney and came out, past Macomber, drying the tip of her nose. The district attorney took her through the office and opened the door for her. She kissed him again and went down the hall. The district attorney closed the door and leaned against it wearily. 'She's got to go to Wisconsin,' he said to Macomber. 'She knows people in Wisconsin. There are lakes. What do you want?'

Macomber explained about Brisbane and Los Angeles and the sheriff's fund and what the county treasurer had said. The district attorney sat down on the bench against the wall and listened with his head down.

'What do you want me to do?' he asked when Macomber finished.

'That Brisbane is a man who should be behind bars for fifteen years. There wouldn't be any doubt about it, once we got him here. He's a known criminal. After all, it would only cost ninety dollars . . . If you said something, if you made a protest . . .'

The district attorney sat on the bench with his head down, his hands loose between his knees. 'Everybody wants to spend money to go some place that isn't Gatlin, New Mexico. You know how much it's going to cost to send my wife to Wisconsin for three weeks? Three hundred dollars. Oh, my God!'

'This is another matter,' Macomber said very softly and reasonably. 'This is a matter of your record. A sure conviction.'

'There's nothing wrong with my record.' The district attorney stood up. 'My record's fine. I got a conviction on that case already. What do you want me to do — spend my life getting convictions on a nine-dollar robbery?'

'If you only said one word to the county treasurer . . . ' Macomber tagged after the district attorney as he started for his inner office.

'If the county treasurer wants to save money, I say, "That's the sort of man we need." Somebody has to save money. Somebody has got to do something else besides supporting the railroads.'

'It's a bad precedent, a guilty man . . . ' Macomber said a little louder than he wanted.

'Leave me alone,' the district attorney said. 'I'm tired.' He went into the inner office and closed the door firmly.

Macomber said, 'Son of a bitch, you bastard!' softly to the imitation oak door, and went out into the marble hall. He bent over and drank from the shining porcelain fountain that the W.P.A. had put there. His mouth felt dry and sandy, with an old taste in it.

Outside he walked down the burning sidewalk, his feet dragging. His belly stretched against the top of his trousers uncomfortably, and he belched, remembering his wife's cooking. In Hollywood he would sit down in a restaurant where the stars ate, no matter what it cost, and have light French dishes, served with silver covers, and wine out of iced bottles. Ninety lousy dollars. He walked in the shade of store-awnings, sweating, wrenching his mind to thought. 'Goddamn it, goddamn it!' he said to himself because he could think of nothing further to do. For the rest of his life, in Gatlin, New Mexico, with never another chance to get even a short breath of joy . . . The back of his eyes ached from thinking. Suddenly he strode out from under the awning, walked up the steps that led to the office of the Gatlin *Herald*.

The city editor was sitting at a big desk covered with dust and tangled copy. He was wearily blue-penciling a long white sheet. He listened abstractedly as Macomber talked, using his pencil from time to time.

'You could show the voters of Gatlin,' Macomber was leaning close over the desk, talking fast, 'what sort of men they got serving them. You could show the property owners of this county what sort of protection they can expect to get from the sheriff, the district attorney, and the county treasurer they put into office. That would make interesting reading-matter, that would, letting men who committed crimes in this county go off thumbing their noses at law enforcement here. If I was you I would write one hell of an editorial, I would. For ninety lousy dollars. One expression of opinion like that in the paper and the sheriff's office would have a man in Los Angeles tomorrow. Are you listening to me?'

'Yeah,' the city editor said, judiciously running his pencil in straight blue lines three times across the page. 'Why don't you go back to being the third deputy sheriff, Macomber?'

'You're a party paper,' Macomber said bitterly, 'that's what's the matter with you. You're Democrats and you wouldn't say anything if a Democratic politician walked off with Main Street in a truck. You're a very corrupt organisation.'

'Yes,' the city editor said. 'You hit the nail on the head.' He used the pencil again.

'Aaah!' Macomber said, turning away. 'For Christ's sake.'

'The trouble with you,' the city editor said, 'is you don't get enough nourishment. You need nourishment.' He poised the pencil thoughtfully over a sentence as Macomber went out, slamming the door.

Macomber walked dully down the street, regardless of the heat beating solidly against him.

He passed his house on the way back to the office. His wife was still sitting there, looking out at the street that was always empty except on Saturday night. Macomber regarded her with his aching eyes, from the other side of the street. 'Is that all you have to do,' he called, 'sit there?'

She didn't say anything, but looked at him for a moment, then calmly glanced up the street.

Macomber entered the sheriff's office and sat down heavily. The sheriff was still there, his feet on the desk.

'Well?' the sheriff said.

'The hell with it.' Macomber dried the sweat off his face with a colored handkerchief. 'It's no skin off my back.' He loosened the laces of his shoes and sat back as the sheriff got Los Angeles on the phone. 'Swanson?' the sheriff said into the phone. 'This is Sheriff Hadley of Gatlin, New Mexico. You can go tell Brisbane he can stop crying. Turn him loose. We're not coming for him. We can't be bothered. Thanks.' He hung up, sighed as a man sighs at the end of a day's work. 'I'm going home to dinner,' he said, and went out.

'I'll stay here while you go home to eat,' the second deputy said to Macomber.

'Never mind,' Macomber said. 'I'm not hungry.'

'O.K.,' the second deputy stood up and went to the door. 'So long, Barrymore.' He departed, whistling.

Macomber hobbled over to the sheriff's swivel chair in his open shoes. He leaned back in the chair, looked up at the poster, 'Wanted for Murder . . . Four Hundred Dollars' lit now by the lengthening rays of the sun. He put his feet into the wastebasket, 'Goddamn Walter Cooper,' he said.

THE GREEK GENERAL

'I did it,' Alex kept saying. 'I swear I did it.'

'Tell me more stories,' Flanagan said, standing right over him, 'I love to hear stories.'

'I swear to God,' Alex said, beginning to feel scared.

'Come on!' Flanagan jerked Alex to his feet. 'We are going to visit New Jersey. We are going to revisit the scene of the crime, except there was no crime.'

'I don't understand,' Alex said hurriedly, putting on his coat and going down the stairs between Flanagan and Sam, leaving his door unlocked. 'I don't understand at all.'

Sam drove the car through the empty night streets, and Alex and Flanagan sat in the back seat.

'I did everything very careful,' Alex said in a troubled voice. 'I soaked the whole goddamn house with naphtha. I didn't forget a single thing. You know me, Flanagan, I know how to do a job . . .'

'Yeah,' Flanagan said. 'The efficiency expert. Alexander. The Greek general. Only the house didn't burn. That's all.'

'I honestly don't understand it.' Alex shook his head in puzzlement. 'I put a fuse into a pile of rags that had enough naphtha on it to wash a elephant. I swear to God.'

'Only the house didn't burn,' Flanagan said stubbornly. 'Everything was dandy, only the house didn't burn. I would like to kick you in the belly.'

'Now, lissen, Flanagan,' Alex protested, 'what would you want to do that for? Lissen, I meant well. Sam,' he appealed to the driver, 'you know me, ain't I got a reputation . . . ?'

'Yeah,' Sam said flatly, not taking his eyes off the traffic ahead of him.

'Jesus, Flanagan, why would I want to run out? Answer me

that, what's there in it for me if I run out? I ask you that simple question.'

'You give me a pain in the belly,' Flanagan said. 'A terrible pain, Alexander.' He took out a cigarette and lit it, without offering one to Alex, and looked moodily out at the policeman who was taking their toll money at the Holland Tunnel entrance.

They rode in silence through the tunnel until Sam said, 'This is some tunnel. It's an achievement of engineering. Look, they got a cop every hundred yards.'

'You give me a pain in the belly, too,' Flanagan said to Sam. So they rode in silence until they came to the skyway. The open starlit sky seemed to loosen Flanagan up a little. He took off his derby and ran his fingers through his sandy hair with a nervous unhappy motion.

'I had to get mixed up with you,' he said to Alex. 'A simple little thing like burning down a house and you gum it up like flypaper. Twenty-five thousand dollars hanging by a thread. Christ!' he said bitterly. 'Maybe I ought to shoot you.'

'I don't understand it,' Alex said miserably. 'That fuse shoulda reached the naphtha in two hours. It shoulda burned like a gas stove.'

'You Greek general.'

'Lissen, Flanagan,' Alex said, tough and businesslike. 'I don't like the way you talk. You talk like I threw the job away on purpose. Lissen, do you think I'd throw five thousand bucks out the window like that?'

'I don't know what you'd do,' Flanagan said, lighting another cigarette. 'I don't think you got enough brains to come in outa the rain. That's my honest opinion.'

'Five thousand bucks is five thousand bucks,' Alex insisted. 'With money like that I could open a poolroom and be a gentleman for the rest of my life.' He looked up at the ceiling of the car and spoke softly. 'I always wanted to operate a poolroom.' Then, harshly, to Flanagan, 'You think I'd give up a chance like that? What do you think – I'm crazy?'

'I don't think nothing,' Flanagan said stubbornly. 'All I know is the house didn't burn. That's all I know.'

He looked stonily out his window and there was quiet in the car as it raced across the Jersey meadows through the stockyard, fertiliser, glue-factory smells, and turned off on the fork to Orangeburg. Two miles out of the town they stopped at an intersection and McCracken came out from behind a tree and got into the car. Sam started the car again even before McCracken was seated. McCracken was not in uniform and there was a harried frown on his face. 'This is the nuts,' McCracken said even before he got the car door closed. 'This is wonderful. This is a beautiful kettle of fish.'

'If you just come to cry,' Flanagan said bluntly, 'you can get right out now.'

'I have been sitting around in the police station,' McCracken wailed, 'and I have been going crazy.'

'All right. All right!' Flanagan said.

'Everything worked just like we planned,' McCracken went right on, pounding his hand on his knee. 'Ten minutes before eleven o'clock an alarm was turned in from the other end of town and the whole damned fire department went charging out to put out a brush fire in a vacant lot. I waited and waited and for two hours there was no sign of a fire from the Little-worth house. Twenty-five thousand bucks!' He rocked back and forth in misery. 'Then I called you. What're you doing, playing a game?'

Flanagan gestured toward Alex with his thumb. 'Look at him. There's the boy. Our efficiency expert. I would like to kick him in the belly.'

'Lissen,' Alex said coolly and reasonably. 'Something went wrong. A mistake. All right.'

'What's all right about it?' McCracken shouted. 'You tell me! Lissen, Alex, I get four thousand bucks a year for bein' Chief of Police of this town, I can't afford to get mixed up in mistakes.'

'I will do the job over,' Alex said soothingly. 'I will do it good this time.'

'You better,' Flanagan said grimly. 'You'll be served up as pie if you make another mistake.'

'That's no way to talk,' Alex said, hurt.

'That's the way I talk,' Flanagan said. 'Sam, go to the Littleworth House.'

The car barely stopped for Alex to jump out in front of the Littleworth house. 'We'll be back in ten minutes,' Flanagan said as he closed the door. 'Find out what went wrong. *Alex!*' he said with loathing.

Alex shrugged and looked back at the huge pile of the Littleworth house, black against the sky. By all rights it should've been just a heap of ashes by now with insurance experts probing in the remains to estimate how much damage was done. Why couldn't it've burned? Alex wept inwardly, why couldn't it? Five thousand dollars, he thought as he went swiftly and quietly across the dark lawn. A nice comfortable poolroom, with the ball clicking like music and the boys buying Coca-Cola at ten cents a bottle between shots and the cash register ringing again and again. A gentleman's life. No wondering every time you saw a cop was he looking for you. Why couldn't it've burned?

He slipped silently through the window that he had left open and padded along the thick carpet to the library, his flashlight winking on and off cautiously in the dark hall. He went directly to the pile of rags in the corner, over which still hung the faint odor of naphtha. He played the flashlight on the fuse that he had carefully lighted before slipping out the window. Only ashes remained. The fuse had burned all right. Uncertainly he touched the rags. They were dry as sand. 'Nuts,' he said softly in the silent library. 'Nuts. Smart guy!' He hit his head with both his hands in irritation. 'What a smart guy!' He kicked the pile of rags bitterly and went back along the hall and jumped out the window and walked out across the lawn and waited for Flanagan and Sam behind a tree, smoking a cigarette.

Alex breathed deeply, looking around him. This was the way to live, he thought, peering at the big houses set behind trees and lawns off in the darkness, fresh air and birds and quiet, going off to Palm Beach when you wanted your house burned down and you didn't want to know anything about it. He sighed, blotting out his cigarette against the tree. A well-run poolroom ought to be good for six, seven thousand dollars a year. You could live very respectable in Flatbush on six, seven thousand dollars a year, there were trees there, all over the place, and squirrels, live squirrels, in the gardens. Like a park, like a real park, that's how people ought to live . . .

The car drew up to him and Flanagan opened the door and leaned out.

'Well, general?' Flanagan asked without humor.

'Look, Flanagan,' Alex said seriously, talking in whispers, 'something went wrong.'

'No!' Flanagan said with bitter irony. 'No! Don't tell me!'

'Do you want to make jokes?' Alex asked. 'Or do you want to hear what happened?'

'For God's sake,' McCracken whispered, his voice tense and high, 'don't be a comedian, Flanagan. Say what you got to say and let's get outa here!' He looked anxiously up and down the street. 'For all I know a cop's liable to come walkin' up this street any minute!'

'Our Chief of Police. Old Iron Nerves,' Flanagan said.

'I'm sorry I ever got into this,' McCracken said hoarsely. 'Well, Alex, what the hell happened?'

'It's very simple,' Alex said. 'I set a two-hour fuse and the naphtha evaporated.'

'Evaporated?' Sam said slowly. 'What's that, evaporated?'

'He's a student, our boy, Alex,' Flanagan said. 'He know. big words. Evaporated. You dumb Greek! You efficiency expert! You stupid sonofabitch! Trust you to burn down a house! Evaporated You ought to be washing dishes! *Alexander!*' Deliberately Flanagan spit at Alex.

'You oughtn't to say that,' Alex said, wiping his face. 'I did my best.'

'What're we going to do now?' McCracken wailed. 'Somebody tell me what we're going to do now.'

Flanagan leaned way over and grabbed Alex fiercely by the collar. 'Lissen, Alexander,' he said right into Alex's face, 'you're goin' back in that house and you're settin' fire to that house, and you're settin' fire to it good! Hear me?'

'Yeah,' Alex said, his voice trembling. 'Sure I hear you, Flanagan. You don't have to tear my collar off. Say, lissen,

Flanagan, this shirt cost me eight bucks . . . '

'You are setting fire to this house personally now,' Flanagan's grip tightened on the collar. 'You are giving this fire the benefit of your personal attention, see? No fuse, no evaporated, nothing, understand?'

'Yeah,' Alex said. 'Sure, Flanagan.'

'You will be served up as pie, anything goes wrong,' Flanagan said slowly, his pale mean eyes glaring straight into Alex's.

'Why don't you leave go my collar?' Alex said, choking a little. 'Lissen, Flanagan, this shirt cost me . . .'

Flanagan spat into his face again. 'I would like to kick you in the belly,' he said. He let go Alex's collar and pushed Alex's face with the heel of his hand.

'Say, Flanagan . . .' Alex protested as he stumbled back.

The car door slammed. 'Move, Sam,' Flanagan said, sitting back.

The car spurted down the street. Alex wiped his face with a shaking hand. 'Oh, Jesus,' he said to himself as he walked back across the completely dark lawn to the house. He heard a sparrow cheep in the three o'clock morning hush and he nearly cried under the peaceful trees.

Once in the house, though, he became very businesslike. He went upstairs to where he had set out buckets of naphtha and brought them down in pairs. He tore down all the drapes from the ground-floor windows and piled them at the farther end of the long hall that ran along one side of the house. Then he took all the linen covers off the furniture and piled them on top of the drapes. He went down to the cellar and brought up three egg boxes full of excelsior and put the excelsior on top of the piled cloth. It made a heap about seven feet high at the end of the hall. He worked grimly, swiftly, ripping cloth when it wouldn't give way easily, running up and down steps, sweating in his overcoat, feeling the sweat roll down his neck on to his tight collar. He soaked every piece of furniture with naphtha, then came out and poured ten gallons of naphtha over the pile at the end of the hall. He stepped back, the acrid smell sharp in his nostrils, and surveyed his work with satisfaction. If that didn't work you couldn't burn this house down in a blast-oven. When he got through with it, the home of the Littleworths would be hot. No mistake this time. He got a broom and broke off the handle and wrapped it heavily with rags. He soaked the rags with naphtha until the liquid ran out of the saturated cloth to the floor. He whistled comfortably under his breath 'There'll be a hot time in the old town tonight' as he opened the window wide behind him at the end of the hall that was opposite the huge pile of cloth and excelsior. It was a narrow hall, but long. A distance of thirty-five feet separated him from the pyre at the other end.

'There'll be a hot time in the old town tonight,' he sang under his breath as he took out a match from the dozen he had lying loose in his pocket. He stood next to the open window, prepared to jump swiftly out as he struck the match, put it to his heavy torch. The torch flared up wildly in his hand and he hurled it with all his strength straight down the hall to the pile of naphtha-soaked cloth and excelsior at the other end. It landed squarely on the pile. For a moment nothing happened. Alex stood, ready at the window, his eyes shining in the fierce light of the flaring torch. Alex smiled and kissed his fingers at the other end of the hall.

Then the whole hall exploded. The pile of cloth became a single huge ball of flame and hurtled down the hall like a flaming shell to the open window behind Alex. With a scream sick in his throat, lost in the immense roar of the exploding house, Alex dove to the floor just as the ball of flame shot over him and through the window to the pull of the open air beyond, carrying his hat and his hair, like smoke going up a chimney to the pull of the sky.

When he came to there was a dusty burned smell in his nostrils. Without surprise he saw that the carpet under his face was quietly afire, burning gently, like coal in a grate. He hit the side of his head three times to put out the fire in what remained of his hair, and sat up dully. Coughing and crying, he dove down to the floor again, escaping the smoke. He crawled along the burning carpet foot by foot, his hands getting black and crisp under him as he slowly made his way to the nearest door. He opened the door and crawled out on to a side porch. Just behind him the hall beams collapsed and a column of flame shot up through the roof, as solid as cement. He sighed and crawled to the edge of the porch and fell off five feet to the loam of a flower bed. The loam was hot and smelled from manure, but he lay there gratefully for a moment, until he realised that something was wrong with his hip. Stiffly he sat up and looked at his hip. Flames were coming out through his overcoat from inside and he could smell his skin broiling. Neatly he unbuttoned his coat and hit at the flames, curling up from the pocket where he had the dozen matches. When he put out the fire on his hip he crawled out to the lawn, shaking his head again and again to clear it, and sat behind a tree. He slid over and went out again, his head on a root.

Far off, far, far off a bell clanged again and again. Alex opened his eyes, singed of their lashes, and listened. He heard the fire trucks turn into the street. He sighed again and crawled, clinging to the cold ground, around the back of the house and through a bare hedge that cut his swelling hands, and away from the house. He stood up and walked off behind a high hedge just as the first fireman came running down toward the back of the house.

Directly, but slowly, like a man walking in a dream, he went to McCracken's house. It took forty minutes to walk there, walking deliberately down alleys and back streets in the dark, feeling the burned skin crack on his knees with every step. He rang the bell and waited. The door opened slowly and McCracken cautiously put his face out.

'My God!' McCracken said and started to slam the door, but Alex had his foot in the way.

'Lemme in,' Alex said in a hoarse broken voice.

'You're burned,' McCracken said, trying to kick Alex's foot out of the doorway. 'I can't have nothing to do with you. Get outa here.'

Alex took out his gun and shoved it into McCracken's ribs. 'Lemme in,' he said.

McCracken slowly opened the door. Alex could feel his ribs

shaking against the muzzle of the gun. 'Take it easy,' McCracken said, his voice high and girlish with fright. 'Lissen, Alex, take it easy.'

They stepped inside the hall and McCracken closed the door. McCracken kept holding on to the doorknob to keep from sliding to the floor from terror. 'What do you want from me, Alex?' His necktie jumped up and down with the strain of talking. 'What can I do for you?'

'I want a hat,' Alex said, 'and I want a coat.'

'Sure, sure, Alex. Anything I can do to help . . .'

'Also I want for you to drive me to New York.'

McCracken swallowed hard. 'Now, look, Alex,' he wiped his mouth with the back of his hand to dry the lips, 'let's be reasonable. It's impossible for me to drive you to New York. I got a four-thousand-dollar job. I'm Chief of Police. I can't take chances like . . .'

Alex started to cry. 'I'll give it to you right in the guts. So help me.'

'All right, Alex, all right,' McCracken said hurriedly. 'What're you crying about?'

'It hurts. I can't stand it, it hurts so much.' Alex weaved back and forth in the hallway in pain. 'I got to get to a doctor before I croak. Come on, you bastard,' he wept, 'drive me to the city!'

All the way to Jersey City Alex cried as he sat there, jolting in the front seat, wrapped in a big coat of McCracken's, an old hat slipping back and forth on his burnt head as the car sped east into the dawn. McCracken gripped the wheel with tight, sweating hands, his face drawn and pale. From time to time he glanced sidewise fearfully at Alex.

'Yeah,' Alex said once when he caught McCracken looking at him. 'I'm still here. I ain't dead yet. Watch where you're goin', Chief of Police.'

A block from the Jersey entrance of the Holland Tunnel, McCracken stopped the car.

'Please, Alex,' he pleaded, 'don't make me take you across to New York. I can't take the chance.'

'I gotta get to a doctor,' Alex said, licking his cracked lips. 'I gotta get to a doctor. Nobody's gonna stop me from getting to a doctor. You're goin' to take me through the tunnel and then I'm goin' to let you have it because you're a bastard. You're an Irish bastard. Start this car. He rocked back and forth in the front seat to help him with the pain. 'Start this car!' he shouted.

Shaking so that it was hard for him to control the car, McCracken drove Alex all the way to the St George Hotel in Brooklyn where Flanagan lived. He stopped the car and sat still, slumped exhausted over the wheel.

'O.K., Alex,' he said. 'Here we are. You're gonna be a good guy, aren't you, Alex, you're not goin' to do anythin' to be sorry for, are you? Remember, Alex, I'm a family man, I'm a man with three children. Come on, Alex, why don't you talk? Why would you want to hurt me?'

'Because you're a bastard,' Alex said painfully because his jaws were stiffening. 'I got a good mind to. You didn't want to help me. I had to make you help me.'

'I got a kid aged two years old,' McCracken cried. 'Do you want to make an orphan of a two-year-old kid? Please, Alex. I'll do anything you say.'

Alex sighed. 'Go get Flanagan.'

McCracken jumped out quickly and came right back with Flanagan and Sam. Alex smiled stiffly when Flanagan opened the door of the car and saw Alex and whistled. 'Nice,' Flanagan said. 'Very nice.'

'Look at him,' Sam said, shaking his head. 'He looks like he been in a war.'

'You ought to a' seen what I done to the house,' Alex said. 'A first-class job.'

'Are you goin' to pass out, Alex?' Sam asked anxiously.

Alex waved his gun pointlessly two or three times and then pitched forward, his head hitting the dashboard with a smart crack, like the sound of a baseball bat on a thrown ball.

When he opened his eyes he was in a dark, meagerly furnished room and Flanagan's voice was saying, 'Lissen, Doc, this man can't die. He's gotta come through, understand? It is too hard to explain away a dead body. It can't be done. I

100

don't care if he loses both legs and both arms and if it takes five years, but he's got to pull through.'

'I should never've gotten mixed up in this,' McCracken's voice wailed. 'I was a damn fool. Risking a four-thousand-dollar-a-year job. I ought to have my head examined.'

'Maybe he will and maybe he won't,' a strange professional voice said. 'That is a well done young man.'

'It looks to me,' Sam's voice said, 'as if he's marked special delivery to Calvary Cemetery.'

'Shut up!' Flanagan said. 'And from now on nobody says a word. This is a private case. Alexander. The lousy Greek.'

Alex heard them all go out before he dropped off again.

For the next five days, the doctor kept him full of dope, and Flanagan kept Sam at his bedside with a towel for a gag, to keep him quiet when the pain became too much to bear. He would start to yell and Sam would shove the towel into his mouth and say soothingly, 'This is a respectable boarding house, Alex. They don't like noise.' And he could scream all he wanted to into the towel and bother no one.

Ten days later the doctor told Flanagan. 'All right. He'll live.'

Flanagan sighed. 'The dumb Greek,' he said, patting Alex on his bandaged head. 'I would like to kick him in the belly. I am going out to get drunk.' And he put on his derby hat, square on his head, and went out.

Alex lay in one position for three months in the furnished room. Sam played nursemaid, feeding him, playing rummy with him, reading the sporting news to him.

At times when Sam wasn't there Alex lay straight on his bed, his eyes half-closed, thinking of his poolroom. He would have a neon sign, 'Alex's Billiard Parlor' going on and off and new tables and leather chairs just like a club. Ladies could play in 'Alex's Billiard Parlor' it would be so refined. He would cater to the better element. Maybe even a refined free lunch, cold meats and Swiss cheese. For the rest of his life he would be a gentleman, sitting behind a cash register with his jacket on. He smiled to himself. When Flanagan gave him his money he would go straight to the pool parlor on

Clinton Street and throw his money down on the counter. Cold cash. This was hard-earned money, he nearly died and there were days he'd wished he could die, and his hair was going to grow in patches, like scrub grass on a highway, for the rest of his life, but what the hell. You didn't get nothing for nothing. Five thousand dollars, five thousand dollars, five thousand dollars . . .

On June first he put on his clothes for the first time in three months and twelve days. He had to sit down after he pulled his pants on because the strain hit him at the knees. He got completely dressed, dressing very slowly, and being very careful with his necktie, and then sat down to wait for Flanagan and Sam. He was going to walk out of that lousy little room with five thousand dollars flat in his wallet. Well, he thought, I earned it, I certainly did earn it.

Flanagan and Sam came in without knocking.

'We're in a hurry,' Flanagan said. 'We're going to the Adirondacks. The Adirondacks in June are supposed to be something. We came to settle up.'

'That's right,' Alex said. He couldn't help but smile, thinking about the money. 'Five thousand dollars. Baby!'

'I think you are making a mistake,' Flanagan said slowly.

'Did you say five thousand dollars?' Sam asked politely.

'Yeah,' Alex said. 'Yeah. Five thousand bucks, that's what we agreed, isn't it?'

'That was in February, Alex,' Flanagan explained calmly. 'A lot of things've happened since February.'

'Great changes have taken place,' Sam said. 'Read the papers.'

'Stop the kiddin',' Alex said, weeping inside the chest. 'Come on, stop the bull.'

'It is true, general,' Flanagan said, looking disinterestedly out the window, 'that you was supposed to get five thousand dollars. But doctor bills ate it all up. Ain't it too bad? It's terrible, how expensive doctors are, these days.'

'We got a specialist for you, Alex,' Sam said. 'Nothing but the best. He's very good on gunwounds too. But it costs.'

'You lousy Flanagan,' Alex shouted. 'I'll get you. Don't

think I won't get you!'

'You shouldn't yell in your condition,' Flanagan said smoothly.

'Yeah,' Sam said. 'The specialist says you should relax.'

'Get out of here,' Alex said through tears. 'Get the hell out of here.'

Flanagan went over to the dresser drawer and took out Alex's gun. Expertly, he broke it and took out the shells and slipped them into his pocket. 'This is just in case your hot Greek blood gets the better of you for a minute, Alex,' he said. 'That would be too bad.'

'Lissen, Flanagan,' Alex cried, 'ain't I going to get anything? Not anything?'

Flanagan looked at Sam, then took out his wallet, threw a fifty-dollar bill at Alex. 'Outa my own pocket,' he said. 'My Irish generosity.'

'Some day,' Alex said, 'I'm going to give it to you. Wait and see. Remember.'

Flanagan laughed. 'The efficiency expert. Look, Alexander, you ought to get out of this business. Take the advice of an older man. You ain't got the temperament for it.'

'I'm going to give it to you,' Alex said stubbornly. 'Remember what I said.'

'The general,' Flanagan laughed. 'The terrible Greek.' He came over and hit Alex's head back with the heel of his hand. 'So long, Alexander.'

He left the room.

Sam came over and put his hand on Alex's shoulder. 'Take care of yourself, Alex,' he said. 'You've been under a big strain.' And he followed Flanagan.

Alex sat for ten minutes, dry-eyed, in his chair. His nose was bleeding a little from Flanagan's push. He sighed and got up and put his coat on. He bent and picked up the fifty-dollar bill and put it in his wallet. He slipped the empty pistol into his topcoat pocket and went out slowly into the warm June sunshine. He walked slowly the two blocks to Fort Greene Park and sat down panting on the first bench. He sat there reflectively for a few minutes, shaking his head sadly from time to time. Finally he took the gun out of his pocket, looked secretly around him, and dropped it into the waste can next to the bench. It fell with a soft dry plop on the papers in the can. He reached into the can and got out a discarded newspaper and turned to the Help Wanted section. He blinked his eyes in the glare of the sun off the newsprint and traced down the page with his finger to 'Help Wanted, Boys.' He sat there in the warm June sunshine, with his topcoat on, making neat little checks with a pencil on the margin of the page.

RESIDENTS OF OTHER CITIES

When the Bolsheviks came, the men of the city, the peasants and clerks and small merchants, hurriedly put on red badges and ran to greet them, singing the half-learned words of the *Internationale*. While they remained in possession of the town there were police on the streets at night and an air of purpose and everyone was called 'Comrade,' even Jews. Then when the Whites recovered the city the men who had not gone with the Bolsheviks ran to greet them and the women hung white sheets out the windows and the houses of the Jews were sacked in pograms and Jews were killed and the young girls were raped by the city's hoodlums. This was in Kiev, in 1918. The city changed hands many times as the war rocked around it, and the full record of those changes could be read in the eyes of the Jewish residents.

The riots started at five o'clock in the evening. All afternoon the men had been gathering silently in the square and in the small inns near by. The peasants came in from the fields, armed with axes, and soldiers of the broken army of the Czar sat at the inn-tables with the rifles with which they had fought the Germans.

We knew they were coming and we hid the silver, the good blankets, the money, and my mother's paisley silk scarf. The whole family gathered at my father's house, all eight children – the four boys and four girls, and my uncle and his wife.

We put out all the lights and locked the door and pulled the blinds and sat all together in the living-room, in the twilight, and even the small children sat still and hushed on the floor. My uncle's wife suckled her four-weeks-old child in the room because it was less fearsome there, with the family assembled. I watched her carefully. She was a handsome woman, my uncle's wife Sara. She was very young, nineteen, and her breast was full but upright. She sang very softly to the child as it fed and that was the only sound in the whole room.

My father sat alone in the center of the room, on his face that same abstract expression as when he led the prayers in the synagogue and looked as though he were engaged directly with God's angels in elevated but intimate discussion. He had a lean scholar's face, my father. He ate very little and was much concerned with spiritual matters and disliked me to a degree because I looked like a peasant, big and broad for my age, and went to the Academy and painted naked women. He caught me looking at my aunt's bare breast and his nostrils widened for a moment and his lip lifted. I watched for another thirty seconds, resisting.

We heard a yell far away, in the still city. The yell died down. The child sighed in my aunt's arms and fell asleep. My aunt covered her breast, sat without moving, watching her husband, my uncle Samuel, pacing slowly up and down between her and the door. A muscle kept tightening and relaxing in Samuel's jaw, making a little white ball and disappearing, again and again. My mother swiftly pulled books down off the shelves, slipped bank notes between their leaves, put them back on the shelves. There were two thousand books on the shelves, in Hebrew, Russian, German, and French. I looked at my watch. It was a quarter to five. The watch was new, a wrist watch, such as army officers wore. I was very proud of it. I wished something would happen. I was sixteen years old.

This is what a pogrom is like. First you hear a yell or two far off. Then the sound of a man running, the steps coming nearer swiftly, the sudden opening and slamming of a door near by. Then a moment later more running and more and more, all silent but for the desperate sound of speed on the street, like leaves swift before a wind. Then silence for a moment and then the mob, approaching, with its single noise.

The mob came up to our house and passed. We didn't look out the window. We didn't say anything. My uncle paced up and down and my aunt looked at him. My father closed his eyes as the mob paused at our house, opened them when the mob passed. My seven-year-old sister, Hester, picked her nose. My mother sat with her hands in her lap.

After a little while we heard a woman weeping outside. The woman walked past our windows and around the corner, weeping.

It was a half an hour before they came. And then they broke the windows with clubs and knocked the door down with axes and in a moment the house was full of men and the street in front of our house was full of men. There was the smell of sweat and the peasant smell of the farm and a little smell of alcohol and there they were, a blur and confusion of faces and coats and guns and knives and axes and bayonets and clubs in the small neat house my mother dusted three times a day. They lighted the lamps and a big man with a mustache, in the uniform of a sergeant of the Czar's army kept yelling, 'Shut up! For Christ's sake, keep your mouths shut!'

We stood huddled in one corner of the room as the big sergeant walked up and down in front of us. My uncle Samuel stood in front of his wife and child and my mother stood in front of my father. Hester cried, the first tears.

The sergeant had a bayonet in his hand and he tapped it on the palm of his other hand. 'The oldest son!' he said. 'Where's the oldest son?'

Hester wept. None of us said anything.

'Well!' the sergeant yelled. He smacked the bayonet down on a table and splinters flew off. 'Goddamnit, where's the stinking oldest son?'

I stepped out. I was sixteen and my brother Eli was older than I and my brother David, but I stepped out.

'What?' I said. 'What?'

The sergeant leaned over. 'Little one,' he pinched my cheek and the men behind him laughed, 'little one, you are now going to make yourself useful.'

I looked at my father. He was watching me thoughtfully, his face abstracted, his eyes narrowed, conversing with the angels.

'What do you want?' I asked. I was facing the whole roomful of men. I could feel the blood passing through my elbows and knees.

The sergeant grabbed me, not very roughly, by the collar. 'Little Jew,' he said, 'we want everything there is in the house. You will take us from room to room and deliver everything.' He shook me. He weighed two hundred and twenty-five pounds.

My mother pushed her way to me. 'Give them as little as you can, Daniel,' she whispered in Yiddish.

The sergeant pushed my mother back. 'Talk Russian,' he said. 'Everybody talk Russian.'

'She doesn't talk Russian,' I said, lying, trying to plan swiftly what I could give them and what I could hold back.

I went from room to room with five of the crowd, growing old, cunning, adept, thoughtful at each step, giving them the things they would have found most easily, some of the silver, some of the blankets, a few small trinkets of my mother's. There were other mobs coming and they, too, would have to be satisfied.

When I passed through the living-room again my uncle Samuel was lying on the floor bleeding from the head and a big peasant was holding the four-weeks-old child in one hand and Sara was in a corner, crying, with men all around her, pulling playfully at her clothes, lifting her skirt. Hester sat on the floor, with her fist in her mouth. My mother sat stolidly, a little fat figure, in front of the glass doors of the bookcase. My father, thin and tall, stood looking dreamily at the ceiling, pulling from time to time at his little beard. The men were laughing and it was hard to hear what anyone was saying and there was broken glass on the carpet already.

In my mother's bedroom I stopped. The men had made a big pile of goods outside in the hall. 'That's all,' I said. 'You got everything.'

The sergeant grinned and pulled my ear. 'You're a nice little boy,' he said. He was enjoying everything. 'You wouldn't lie to me, would you?'

'No.'

108

'You know what happens to little boys who lie to me, don't you?'

'Yes. You're hurting my ear.'

'Oh.' The sergeant turned to the men behind him with broad concern. 'I'm hurting his ear. I'm damaging the poor little Jewboy's ear. Isn't that too bad?'

The men laughed. There was laughter throughout the house. All the mobs that came to our house made the house ring with their laughter.

'Maybe if I cut it off,' the sergeant said, 'maybe it wouldn't hurt so much. What do you say, boys?'

The boys agreed. 'A nice kosher ear,' one of them said. 'For stew.'

'You're absolutely sure, now,' the sergeant said, twisting my ear, 'that there's nothing left?'

'Yes,' I said.

'I hope you're right, little boy. For your sake.'

We marched down through the living room and to the small music room right next to it. There were sliding doors between the living room and the music room. 'We are now going to search the house, little boy,' the sergeant said very loudly. He had a voice you could hear over all the noise. 'And if we find anything you haven't shown us, if we find one little silver baby spoon . . . ' He touched my throat with the bayonet. I felt the blood come to the skin, drip in a little trickle to my collar. 'The end. Poor little Jewboy.' The sergeant looked significantly at my mother. She looked back at him firmly. My two older brothers David and Eli, pale and spiritual-looking, like my father, stood together, holding each other's hands. David's eyes were open very wide and there were white lines, like ridges, across his cheeks. They watched me intently, never taking their eyes off me.

The sergeant marched me into the music room after ordering the men to search the house. The sergeant closed the doors firmly. 'Sit down, little boy,' he said. I sat down and he sat down opposite me, the bayonet across his knee. 'One little silver baby spoon,' he said. 'Sssst!'

I didn't feel that he could kill me. He was a foolish, lumpy man, with spit sliding down his chin. I had read books on French art, I knew what Impressionism was, I had seen reproductions of the paintings of Cézanne and Renoir. It was impossible that a big fool with a torn and muddy uniform could kill me.

'You're still sure there's nothing else?'

'You got the last piece.'

'All Jews should be killed,' he said. I looked at the bayonet and thought of the searchers passing the bookcase with the rubles hidden in every other book, passing the trunk with the false bottom in the attic, the coal pile hiding the samovar in the cellar, the lace in the samovar . . .

'Russia is ridden by Jews,' the sergeant said, grinning. 'It is this country's great plague. I fought at Tannenburg, I'm entitled to have opinions.'

Sara started screaming outside in the living room and I heard my father start to pray.

'We will kill the Jews,' the sergeant said, 'and then the Bolsheviks. I suppose you're a Bolshevik.'

'I'm a painter,' I said. I said it proudly, even then.

'Well,' said the sergeant, speaking loudly, because Sara was screaming, 'a little boy like you.' He picked up my hand and saw my wrist watch. 'That's just what I've been looking for,' he said. He tore it off my wrist and dropped it into his pocket. 'Thank you, little one.' He grinned.

I felt very bad. That wrist watch made me a gentleman, a citizen of the world.

He took out a pack of cigarettes, took one, automatically offered the pack to me. I had never smoked before, but I took one. I smoked it, feeling suddenly a man, thinking of what my father would say if he saw me now, smoking. None of us smoked in our house, not even my uncle. Well, I thought, no matter what, I know what it is to smoke. I didn't inhale the smoke. I pushed it around my mouth and hurriedly blew it out.

'The painter,' the sergeant said, 'the little artist. Are you having a good time, Mr Artist?'

He was a very cruel man, that sergeant.

'Maybe they're opening a closet door downstairs,' the sergeant said, patting my knee, 'and maybe they see candle-sticks there, gold candlesticks.'

'They don't see anything,' I said, crying all of a sudden because the smoke whirled up in my eyes. 'There's nothing to see.'

'Little artist, little Jew painter.' He cut the buttons off my coat one by one with the bayonet. He was having a very good time. Hester and Sara were both screaming in the living room. The door opened and two of the searchers came in.

'Nothing,' said one of them, 'not a stinking button.'

'Lucky little boy,' the sergeant said to me. He leaned over, smiling, and hit me on the temple, with his fist. I fell over and the room and the noise went far, far away.

When I came to, my head was in my mother's lap, and the men had gone. I opened my eyes and saw Sara in my uncle Samuel's arms, with the blood still coming slowly from the wound in his head and staining their clothes and they not noticing it all, but just standing there, clutched together with-out tears, their hands digging into each other's shoulders. The baby was lying on the chair next to them sleeping. My mother's face was calm over me and her voice came down distantly, 'Daniel, little Daniel, lion-hearted Daniel, everything is all right, sweetheart, everything is all right.'

In the distance I heard my father. 'The most profound mis-take of my life,' he was saying. 'I had an opportunity to go to America in 1910. Why didn't I go? Why in the name of the Almighty God, didn't I go?'

'Don't move, baby,' my mother said softly. 'Lie there and close your eyes.'

'I ought to be ashamed of myself,' I heard my brother David's voice, bitter, full of tears, 'I am the oldest son. And he stepped forward. I'm nineteen and he's sixteen and I stayed behind. God forgive me.'

'Little Daniel,' my mother crooned, her hand going lightly over my forehead, 'little Daniel with the brains of a philo-sopher.' She was chuckling. In the middle of all the blood and tears she was chuckling. I sat up and laughed, too, and she

111

kissed me.

Outside, from the other side of the city, we heard shots and nearer a man screamed and we heard horses galloping down the next street.

'Maybe it's the Bolsheviks,' my mother said. 'Maybe we're saved.'

'Let us pray,' said my father. Everyone arranged himself for prayer, even my uncle Samuel. He gently took Sara's arms down from his shoulders and kissed her hands. He bent down and picked up his hat and put it on. Sara sat with the child in her arms, the fright draining from her eyes. The men hadn't really hurt her.

My father started to pray. I didn't believe in my father's prayers. My father was always at the side of God and he neglected life. I hated this insane holiness, this neglect of flesh, the denial of the present for eternity.

I stood up and went to the window when my father began, 'Blessed Father, God Almighty . . . '

He stopped. 'Daniel,' he called. 'We are praying.'

'I know,' I said. My brothers and sisters looked nervously at me. 'I want to look out the window. I don't want to pray.'

I could hear the breath whistle into the lungs of my brothers.

My father's lip twisted. 'Daniel,' he began . . . then he stopped and shrugged and looked up at his angels. 'Blessed Father,' he started the prayer, 'God Almighty . . . '

My brothers chimed in with the responses.

I smiled to myself at the window. This was the first time I had ever refused my father. 'The oldest son,' they had asked, and I had stepped out and said, 'What?' Now I could announce to my father, 'I don't want to pray.'

I listened to the shots in the distance and the shrieks and the solid noise of the crowds and I smiled at the window.

In the next two days the mobs came to our house nineteen times. In the middle of all the screams, all the laughter, all the terror and devastation, I kept a careful, crazy account. They have been here nine times, here they come again, there are still two silver candy dishes in the cellar we can give them, this makes

112

the tenth time, will they kill somebody this time, ten, remember ten, the next time will be the eleventh.

The house was completely gutted. All the windows were broken, all the doors had been torn off to make fires in the streets, all the mirrors had been smashed, the carpets ripped up and carried out with the furniture. The last bit of hidden food had been found and stolen, the last blanket and loose piece of clothing. The mobs had broken into liquor stores by the second night and the men came rushing in reeking of alcohol, louder, more and more violent. Death came nearer and nearer with each visit, the eleventh time, the twelfth time, the heavy muddy boots, the shouts the drunken songs, the men standing, swaying a little in front of my father and my uncle, prodding them with bayonets, waiting for a sign of resistance, of violence, a call of encouragement from their friends, to start the business of killing. They played joyously with death, always on the thin edge of it, sniffing it as the ultimate satisfaction of the carnival, calling it near, allowing it to retreat, postponing it for another time, the way a child postpones a sweet.

They twice stripped my aunt Sara and my oldest sister Rachel completely of their clothes and made them stand there, upright, in the broken-windowed house, on the glass-strewn floor, with all to see, but they went no further and we wrapped Sara and Rachel in rags and for the first time my mother wept.

All night we saw the flare of burning houses outside our windows and all night we heard the sounds of scattered shots and all night, the screams.

The women huddled in the cold, on the floor, and cried and the children sobbed and my brother David kept walking up and down yelling, 'The next time, I'll kill one of them! I swear to God!'

'Sssh,' said my father. 'You'll kill no one. That's not your business. Let them kill, not you.'

'I'd like them to kill me,' David shouted. 'Let me kill one of them first, then let them kill me! It's better than this.'

'Sssh,' said my father. 'God's will be done. They will suffer finally.'

'Oh, my God!' David said.

'Why didn't I go to America in 1910?' my father asked, rocking back and forth. 'Why didn't I?'

My uncle Samuel sat by the window holding his child, looking first down the street for new mobs, then at his wife Sara, stretched in the corner, in her rags, her face turned hopelessly to the wall. The blood had dried on Samuel's face and he had neglected to wipe it off and it made a pattern on his cheek like rivers on a map. His beard was coming out heavily on his face and his eyes had gone deep into his head and his cheeks had collapsed along the bones of his jaw. Occasionally he bent over and kissed his child, sleeping in his arms.

I sat with my arms around my brother Eli, with Hester between us, to keep warm. They had taken my jacket and I was stiff with cold and I lay there with my eyes wide open remembering, listening, tonight's tears, yesterday's, tomorrow's.

'Go to sleep, Hester, little Hester,' I said softly from time to time when Hester would awake. Every time she woke she began to sob, immediately, as though that were the way nature had made little children, sleep quiet, awake weeping.

Vengeance, I thought, listening to the women of my family cry; feeling the bruises stiffen where I had been beaten, sighing, as I moved and cuts opened and bled into my clotted clothes, vengeance, vengeance.

'They're coming again,' my uncle Samuel said, from his place at the window, just before daybreak. We heard the well-recognised sound of the mob coming nearer. 'I'm not going to stay here,' Samuel said. 'The hell with it. Sara, Sara, darling,' he said more gently than any man I have ever heard use a woman's name. 'Come, Sara . . .'

Sara stood up and took his arm.

'What should we do?' my mother asked.

My father looked up at his angels. 'Come,' I said, taking my place in command, 'let's try the streets.'

We filed out through the back door, twelve of us walking, Samuel carrying the child in his arms. We trailed through the icy mud, keeping close to walls, walking, walking, avoiding the sounds of life, fleeing from lights, hating every five minutes to allow the children to rest, running across open streets like rabbits across a bare field.

Vengeance, I thought, leading the march along back alleys, behind fences, death, fire and torture. I held my mother's hand. 'Keep going, Momma, please, Momma,' I yelled at her as she stumbled in the mud. 'You must, Momma.'

'Yes, Daniel, of course, Daniel,' she said, gripping my hand in her calloused, work-scarred hands. 'Excuse me for going so slow, kindly excuse me.'

'Cleveland,' my father said, as the sun came up. 'I could have gone to Cleveland. My uncle invited me.'

'Keep quiet, Poppa! Please, please don't talk about America!' David said.

'Yes,' said my father. 'Of course. What's done is . . . God's will. Who am I,' he said, leaning against a wall as we stopped for a moment, 'who am I to question . . . ? Still, in America these things do not happen and I had the opportunity . . .'

David didn't say any more.

It became harder to keep out of the mob's way as it grew lighter. Nobody in Kiev seemed to sleep all those two days and our escapes became closer and closer. Twice we were shot at from windows and we ran slithering in the mud, with the children screaming, to take protection behind the corners of houses. The third time we were shot at my brother David turned around with his mouth open and sat down in the mud.

'In the knee,' he said. 'My knee . . .'

My mother and I ripped the sleeve off my father's jacket and tied it around David's leg above the knee. My father stood there, watching us, looking lopsided and peculiar, standing there with one sleeve. I put David over my back and we started back to the house. He tried to keep from yelling by pounding me in the back with his fists as I lurched and the knee knocked against me.

When we got back to the house we sat once more in the destroyed living room. The sun streamed in and it looked mad and unfamiliar and impossible, with all of us sitting there on the floor in the broad daylight, with Rachel and Sara wrapped in rags like mummies, and my father with one sleeve and

David with the sleeve knotted around his leg and the sweat coming off him and making little pools on the floor. The children sat all together in a corner, terribly quiet, watching each movement of the adults with quick movements of their eyes.

All day long the mobs kept coming and each time they brought death a little closer, each time the bayonet prods went a little deeper, each time more blood was shed. David became hysterical late in the afternoon and fell into trances and rigid fits and there was nothing to do but sit there and listen to him and look at each other like insane animals in a lunatic zoo.

'You can blame this on me,' my father kept saying. 'I had the opportunity and I was not the man to grasp it. The truth. I am not a strong man. I'm a scholar. I did not want to cross the ocean to a country with a foreign language. Blame me. Everybody blame me.'

At four o'clock Eli got up. 'I'm going out,' he said. 'I can't stand it here.'

Before he could be stopped he turned and ran down the street.

Just at nightfall a mob came with torches. They filled the house. They were in dangerous high spirits, full of whisky and blood.

They ranged the house, came back to the living room disappointed because there was nothing left to be looted.

They held all the men, two to each one of us and stood in front of us, trying to devise new pleasures. This was the time, I thought, this is where we die, there is nothing left. I didn't want to die.

And this time we nearly did die, but one of the members of the mob spoke up, 'Shave him, shave the old holy bastard!'

The mob met this with roars of approval and two men pulled my father out to the center of the room and in the flaring light of the torches a little fat man began to shave him with a bayonet. The fat man did it with elaborate comic flourishes, holding my father's chin in arched fingers and standing off with cocked head to admire his handiwork while

116

the men behind him laughed uproariously.

Finally, my father wept. The tears streamed down his cheeks and gleamed on the bayonet that was shaving his soft trim black beard off his face.

When the job was done, they threw my father to the floor and left in good spirits, singing.

My father sat in the new silence on the floor, bleeding and strangely naked in my eyes, with his suddenly girlish mouth and soft chin and his eyes staring wild and frightened and helpless, imploring the angels now, not regarding them any longer as magnificent equals.

'The next time,' I said, trying to sound very businesslike and unemotional among these wild and feverish animals of my family, 'the next time they will kill us. Let's get into the streets in the dark. Please . . . Please . . .'

I carried David and my mother led my father by the hand as we stepped out of our house.

As we started down the street, the door of the tailor's shop across the street opened and our neighbor, Kirov, the tailor, came out. He was not a Jew and his shop hadn't been touched. He was a big fat man of thirty-two or three, already bald. He crossed the street to us and silently shook my father's hand.

'Terrible,' he said. 'Wild animals. The times, the times, who would ever have thought we would see times like this in Kiev?'

My father kept pumping his hand again and again, unable to talk.

'Where're you going?' Kirov asked.

'No place,' I told him. 'We're going to walk up and down in the streets.'

'Jesus Christ!' Kirov said, stroking Hester's head. 'Impossible! I can't believe, I can't . . . Come, come with me, all of you. In my house nobody'll bother you and you can wait until this has blown over. Come. Not another word!'

My mother looked at me and I looked at her and we smiled crookedly at each other.

Kirov helped me with David and in five minutes we were all

117

in his house, lying once more on the floor in the dark, but for the first time in two days with a feeling of safety.

I even fell asleep and awoke only for an instant when I heard a door open and close in the house. I slept without dreams, without the past, the future, without vengeance, or wonder that I was still alive or might survive this time. I slept and the children slept and my mother slept next to me in my father's arms and Sara slept in Samuel's arms, with their child beside them.

Somebody kicked me and I opened my eyes and looked up in the light and there was Kirov and there was the mob and Kirov was smiling and I realised suddenly that he had lived for eight years as a neighbor across the street from us, saying 'Good morning' every day and 'Isn't this a wonderful spring day?' and mending our clothes and for eight years he had nursed a secret hatred and the last two days had touched it off in him and here he was with a mob he had collected himself, and this was going to be the worst.

I sat up. The lights were on in the room and I saw my family awakening, deep out of the pit of sleep, bit by bit take in the silent grinning men standing around us, bit by bit awaken to terror and hopelessness.

Kirov had brought all the men of his family, his two brothers, big heavy men, and even his old father, toothless, limping, grinning like the rest of them.

'Mr Kirov,' my mother said. 'What do you want from us? We have nothing left. Nothing by rags. You have been our neighbor for eight years and we have never had a harsh word . . .'

One of Kirov's brothers grabbed Sara and ripped the rags off her and I saw what the men had come for, what we had left. Kirov himself grabbed my sister Rachel, seventeen years old, but slim and unformed, like a child.

My uncle Samuel sprang at Kirov's brother and hit him across the face and a man standing behind him stabbed Samuel through with a bayonet. Samuel's hand clutched Sara, then relaxed and the man behind him pulled the bayonet out and

Samuel fell down. He got up to one knee again and Kirov's brother took the bayonet and put it through Samuel's throat and left it there as Samuel fell.

I saw what happened after that. Everybody else closed his eyes, my mother, my father, David, even the children. My father's lips moved in prayer and he kept his eyes tightly shut, but I saw what happened.

I kept alive by planning, with cold reason and ingenuity, torture, mutilation, horror, for the men in that room. Torture by knife and fire and whip, applied with my own hands, making sure to hurt each man most in his most vulnerable spot. I market each man in that room and remembered each man in that room.

I don't know how long the men would have stayed but soon from the streets came cries of, 'Bolsheviks! The Reds! They're coming! They're entering the city! The Reds! Long live the Soviets!'

Kirov put out the lights hurriedly and there was a confused scurrying and trampling around. I opened a window and dropped to the ground and went running toward the cries. Soon I was among a whole crowd of men and women, running, running to greet the victorious army. I felt the tears flow bitterly, like iron, down my cheeks as I ran and I saw that in that crowd of people there were many others weeping as they ran.

We turned a corner and there was the vanguard of the triumphant Red Army, marching into Kiev. They were in rags, many of them, and bearded and cheerful and some of them were in uniform and some weren't and some had shoes and some didn't and there was one soldier in a butcher's apron who carried only a huge cavalry saber for armament and they were all eating fruit compote out of cans from a grocery store they had passed on the way into town, but they marched in, fighting men who had won the town fairly, and men and women alike flung themselves at the soldiers and kissed them as they marched.

'Captain!' I stopped the man who seemed to be in command. He was a small man who looked like a clerk. He was very busy as he walked along, spearing a peach with his bayonet out of the can. 'Captain, please . . . '

'What do you want?' He started walking again, after stopping for a moment, still fishing for the peach.

'I want a gun, Captain, I must have a gun, and some soldiers!' I was crying and I dug my fingers into his arm: 'Listen to me, for God's sake, listen to me!'

'How old are you, comrade?' He kept walking, eating the peach now.

'Sixteen. Please, please give me a gun and some soldiers . . . '

'Go home, little comrade,' he said, patting me on the head, 'go home to your momma and tomorrow when we've all had some sleep and everything is nicely organised you come around to headquarters and everything will be . . . '

'I can't wait until tomorrow!' The tears kept coming. 'Now! Tonight! I must have the gun tonight!'

'Whom do you want to shoot?' he stopped and examined me for the first time.

'There are fifteen men I . . . '

'God almighty, comrade!' He laughed.

'What're you laughing at?' I yelled. 'What the hell do you mean by laughing?'

He wiped his face wearily. 'I'm so tired, comrade. We've been fighting for two weeks and I want to lie down.'

'Goddamn you!' I cried. 'Why don't you listen to me?'

He sighed and put his arm around me and we walked close together. 'All right, little boy,' he said. 'Is it as bad as you think?'

I told him. His face became very grave and he threw away the compote can and gripped my shoulder twice. He took me to a very large man with a uniform jacket but ordinary pants who was marching a few paces back. This was the Cheka officer who was to set up police in Kiev immediately.

The Captain talked to him, still holding me by the shoulder. The Cheka officer sighed. 'I can give you one man,' he said. 'I hope he can keep awake long enough to get to the house.'

'And a gun! I want a gun!' I yelled. 'A rifle for me, don't forget that!'

Both the men looked queerly at me, then at each other. 'He's sixteen years old,' the Captain said. 'Sure,' the Cheka officer said softly, 'we'll give you a rifle. Now, for Christ's sake, will you stop bawling?'

'Yes,' I said, though the tears didn't stop. 'Don't mind that. Where's the gun?'

The Cheka officer gave me his rifle and called to a soldier. 'Go with this young man,' the Cheka officer said. 'There is a little police work to be done. He knows what to do, the young man. Please stop crying . . . what's your name?'

'Daniel,' I said. 'I'm not crying. Thank you very much.'

We started off, the soldier and I. He was a very tall, wide soldier, a very young one, too. His eyes were almost closed and there were dark circles under them as though he had been punched neatly there.

'Long live the revolution, Daniel!' the Captain yelled after me. 'Long live Lenin!'

'Yes,' I called back. Then, to the soldier, 'Please, comrade, walk faster!'

'I'm very sleepy,' the soldier said. 'I want very much to lie down.'

When we got back to Kirov's house, only my family were there, grouped silently around my uncle Samuel's body. Sara and Rachel lay face down on the floor with two of Kirov's blankets over them. Rachel was sobbing, but Sara lay without a sound, without movement, clutching her baby. The men had disappeared.

'Where are they?' I asked as I came through the door. 'Where're the Kirovs?'

My father looked soberly at the rifle in my hand.

'Daniel,' he said, 'what are you doing with a gun?'

'Where're the Kirovs?' I yelled.

My father shook his head. Already the distant light of God and His angels was coming back into his eyes.

'Tell me! Tell me!' I screamed.

'They are not here,' my father said. 'That is sufficient. They will not bother us any more. The trouble is over. God has punished us and He has lifted the punishment. Let that be enough. It is not our part to punish.'

'You damned fool!' I screamed.

'Listen,' said the soldier, 'I've got to get some sleep.'

'Momma!' I appealed to my mother. 'Momma, I got a gun, tell me where they are!'

My mother looked at my father. He shook his head. My mother took my hand. 'They're in the cellar of our house. Six of them. The old man couldn't run, he has a bad leg, old man Kirov.'

'Shame!' said my father. 'What're you doing?'

'All the Kirovs?' I asked. 'Are they there?'

My mother nodded.

'Come on,' I said to the soldier. We ran down the steps and across the street to my own house. I found a candle in the kitchen and the soldier lit it and held it for me. I threw open the door of the cellar and went down the steps. There, against the far wall, crouched six men. The four Kirovs, a cousin of theirs, and the man who had stabbed my uncle Samuel, still holding his bayonet.

When he saw us standing there with guns he threw his bayonet down. It made a dry, shuffling noise on the dirt floor.

'We didn't do anything,' Kirov the tailor cried to the soldier. 'As Jesus is my Judge!'

'We were just hiding here to avoid getting caught in the fighting,' old man Kirov said. His nose was running but he paid no attention to it.

'We're Reds,' the owner of the bayonet cried. 'Long live Lenin!'

'Long live Lenin!' they all shouted.

Their voices abruptly dropped when my mother and father and Sara appeared and came down the steps.

The soldier just stood there, his eyes almost closed, holding his rifle loosely, yawning, wide tremendous yawns from time to time.

My mother and father and Sara stood behind us silently. Sara held her baby at her throat. Her eyes were dry.

'Long live the Revolution!' old man Kirov called finally,

his voice thin and quavery in the wet cellar.

'Well,' said the soldier, 'these the ones?'

'Yes,' I said.

'We didn't do anything!' Kirov the tailor cried. 'So help me, Jesus!'

'These are not the men,' my father said. 'These are old friends. The men you want ran away.'

'Who's this?' the soldier asked.

'My father.'

'Well, who's right?' The soldier looked blearily at my father.

'The old man!' Kirov the tailor shouted. 'We have been neighbors for eight years!'

'Those are the men,' my mother said quietly.

Old man Kirov finally wiped his nose. I laughed.

'Idiot!' my father said bitterly to my mother. 'You are storing up more trouble. "Those're the men" you say. Today they're arrested. Tomorrow the Whites come in, they are free. Then what'll happen to us?'

'Those're the men,' my mother said.

'Who's she?' The soldier yawned.

'My mother.'

'Those're the men,' Sara said. Her voice was very low and broken, as though these were her last words and after them she would discard forever the instrument of speech.

'Well?' I asked the soldier. 'Are you satisfied?'

'I'm satisfied,' he said.

I fired the gun into the dirt wall of the cellar.

All heads but the soldier's jerked with the noise, immense in that small low room. The smell of the powder was sharp in our noses. I sneezed.

'What're you going to do?' my father asked, his voice trembling.

I pulled the bolt of the gun, throwing the spent cartridge, putting in the fresh one. 'Is that how you do it?' I asked.

'That's how,' the soldier answered. He stood there impersonally ragged, spent, just.

'What are you going to do?' Kirov the tailor asked.

I shot him through the head. He died as he fell. He was only eleven feet away.

The other men shrank against the wall, but separately, trying to put as much space as possible between themselves and the next man.

'Daniel!' my father shouted. 'I forbid you! You must not have their blood on your hands! Daniel!'

I shot the tailor's older brother.

The old man Kirov began to cry. He fell to his knees and put his hands out toward me and said, 'Daniel, Daniel, little boy . . .' I remembered what I had seen in the lighted room in his son the tailor's house, I remembered the old man, toothless and chuckling and my aunt Sara. I shot him as he kneeled.

My father started to sob and ran up the steps. Sara and my mother stood behind me. The soldier rubbed his eyes to keep them open. I felt, in a way, happy, though bitterly happy.

I pulled the bolt.

'Forgive me, forgive me,' wept the youngest Kirov. 'I didn't know what I . . .'

I pressed the trigger. He wheeled around and fell across his father.

I pulled the bolt and aimed carefully at the next man. He was standing there, calmly, rubbing his nose, looking at the ceiling. I pressed the trigger, but nothing happened.

'You need a new clip,' the soldier said. He gave me a new clip and opened the magazine for me and I put the clip in and aimed once more at the next man. He was still rubbing his nose and looking at the ceiling and it was a little surprising to see him die.

The bayonet owner rushed at me as I was pulling the bolt for the last shot and brushed past me and ran up the steps. I ran after him and out into the street. I fired at him and somehow hit him and he fell. He got up again and ran again and I ran after him and shot again. Once more he fell. More slowly this time, he reeled to his feet and stumbled on. I had plenty of time to go after him and take careful aim. This was the most satisfactory moment, the wavering, bloody figure, arms out directly in the rifle's sights. This time he fell, raised himself once on his hand, then dropped into the mud for good.

I stood there with the rifle getting warm in my hand. I felt disappointed and cold and let down. This had not been the deep pleasure I had imagined in Kirov's room. The balances were not even. They had died too easily. They had not suffered enough pain. They had come off best in the bargain, finally.

The soldier came over and I gave him the rifle. Then I began to cry again. He patted me on the head. 'All right, little comrade,' he said. Then he trudged off with two rifles to get some sleep.

My mother and Sara came and let me into the house.

My father wouldn't talk to me after that, and after we had buried my uncle Samuel and sat for a week in proper mourning, during which my father didn't look at me once, I decided to move on. I was restless and changed anyway and I couldn't live in my father's home any more as a schoolboy and I left.

The Reds lost Kiev again and it was a long time before the war was over and before I saw any of my family again and by that time my father was dead.

RICH MAN, POOR MAN
by Irwin Shaw

From the author of THE YOUNG LIONS and TWO WEEKS IN ANOTHER TOWN comes the greatest novel to appear in post-war America. Truly global in the scope of its humanity and passion, RICH MAN, POOR MAN is the story of a generation at war with the values of its past, the hypocrisy and tension of its present and the terrifying inevitability of a shipwrecked future.

Rudolph is the romantic, who learns to live with doubt and make a fortune at 30. His brother Tom is the brute, whose acid-scarred American dream is coloured with boiling blood. Their sister, Gretchen, seduced by the small town's leading citizen, is the beauty in urgent search of a man – the only man – who can save her from herself.

'By the end of it we know America from coast to coast.'
— **Daily Telegraph**

NEW ENGLISH LIBRARY

BEGGARMAN, THIEF
by Irwin Shaw

HERE IS the book that everyone has been waiting for for seven years – the sequel to *Rich Man, Poor Man*. Continuing in masterly style the saga of the Jordache family, Irwin Shaw fills a huge canvas, moving with consummate skill between Europe and America, as he pursues the fortunes – the joys and sorrows, the successes and failures – of each member of the family.

NEW ENGLISH LIBRARY

IRWIN SHAW

Acceptable Losses	£1.95
Beggarman, Thief	£2.95
Bread Upon The Waters	£2.50
Evening in Byzantium	£1.60
Lucy Crown	£1.95
Rich Man, Poor Man	£2.95
The Top of the Hill	£2.50
The Troubled Air	£1.50
Two Weeks in Another Town	£2.50
The Young Lions	£2.95

All these books are available at your local bookshop or newsagent, or can be ordered direct from the publisher. Just tick the titles you want and fill in the form below.

Prices and availability subject to change without notice.

NEL BOOKS, P.O. Box 11, Falmouth TR10 9EN, Cornwall.

Please send cheque or postal order, and allow the following for postage and packing:

U.K. – 55p for one book, plus 22p for the second book, and 14p for each additional book ordered to a £1.75 maximum.

B.F.P.O. & EIRE – 55p for the first book, plus 22p for the second book, and 14p per copy for the next 7 books, 8p per book thereafter.

OTHER OVERSEAS CUSTOMERS – £1.00 for the first book, plus 25p per copy for each additional book.

Name ....

Address...

....

Title..